Secret Desire

Secret Temptations, Volume 3

Cameron Hart

Published by Cameron Hart, 2024.

SECRET DESIRE

First edition. June 27, 2024.

ISBN: 979-8227430618

Written by Cameron Hart.

Want a free book?

Sign up for my newsletter[1] and get your free copy of Chasing Stacy!

One look at the stunning waitress carrying the weight of the world on her shoulders, and I'm a goner. I wasn't looking for a sweet little thing with auburn hair and more baggage than I can fit on the back of my bike, but there's no going back now. She's mine. I'll prove to her I'm more than capable of handling her past and making her feel safe again.

---

1. https://dl.bookfunnel.com/7wbqvhsx8r

Chapter 1

Josephine

"Are you sure this isn't a little... too much?" I ask Jen, one of my roommates. She stops digging through my dresser long enough to turn around and give me a once-over.

"You look great," she encourages. "Classy and sophisticated, but not snobby."

I look at my reflection in the half mirror above my dresser, taking in the black pencil skirt that hits right below my knees, the lacy white cami, and the loose-fitting silk teal blouse I paid way too much for. I need to nail this interview, and I wanted to look the part. I convinced myself it was an investment in my future, but now that I'm looking at eating Ramen for the next month, I'm not so sure.

However, what's done is done, and I need to accept that. I try not to have any regrets in life, so I push the buyer's remorse aside and attempt a cordial, polite smile. Jen snorts out a laugh, and I roll my eyes at her. "I'm just getting into character," I inform her, right before sticking my tongue out.

"Uh-huh," she says dubiously. "You might have to work on that a bit. Oh! Yes, this is what I was looking for!" Jen twirls around, holding out a familiar butterfly brooch. "For good luck."

I give her a watery smile, blinking back tears as I take the brooch. It was my mother's favorite piece of jewelry. She had more expensive, older, and far more impressive pieces, but I picked out this one for her when I was little. My fingers glide across the tiny blue crystals and purple gems that make up the butterfly's body, then trace the golden edges of the wings. "Thanks," I whisper.

My parents passed away thirteen years ago, and I have hardly anything to remember them by. I was shuffled around foster homes for a few years and lost nearly everything precious to me in the process. I've learned to either not have valuables or protect them with my life. This butterfly brooch survived all these years, so I've dubbed it my lucky charm.

Fiddling the clip open, I thread it through the material of my blouse, adjusting the brooch so it rests on my left shoulder, just below my collarbone. It's a little gaudy, but that makes it perfect. A little sparkle never hurt anyone. Plus, it'll make me stand out amongst the other candidates, right? I hope so. I need this job.

"Hey," Jen says, bringing me back into the moment. "This is the perfect job for you. A nanny to a cute little girl? You're going to kill it!"

"I better," I huff out bitterly.

Just then, the front door to our three-bedroom apartment opens, followed by what sounds like shoes being kicked off. I roll my eyes, knowing I'll have to walk past our other roommate, Ashley, on the way out.

"Forget her," Jen says sternly. "Seriously, she's not worth wasting your breath on. I still can't believe she got you fired from Salem's Boutique."

"Oh, my god, I know!" I'm geared up to talk shit about Ashley and blame her for all of my life's problems, but then I take a breath and refocus. Life is short. Too short to hold on to grudges. Do I like Ashley? Hell, no. But do I want to spend the rest of my life stewing over how she stole clothes and jewelry from my place of work and got me fired? Definitely not. Especially since Ashley doesn't care one bit.

"Not to add any pressure," Jen says as she straightens my blouse and picks away little fuzzies from my skirt. "But I need you to get this job. You can't leave me alone with Ashley!"

"Yeah, well, I need this job so I'm not homeless when the rent is due," I mutter.

Jen's shoulders drop, and I feel like a jerk. She's a good friend but a little self-centered. We met in a group home in foster care and aged out together, along with Ashley. Jen and I have always been close, but

Ashley mostly hung around us because she knew we were looking for a third roommate when we got out.

"Right. I'm sorry."

"No, Jen, I'm sorry. That wasn't fair of me to snap at you."

Jen gives me a grin. "You've got such a tender heart, you know? It's kind of surprising considering everything we've been through."

I shrug, not sure what to say to that. It's not the first time someone has called me tenderhearted. I don't understand why that always seems to be a weakness. People who put up walls to keep others out only end up hurt, isolated, and bitter. I've had enough pain and loneliness to last a lifetime, so I try to keep my heart open for whatever is next. Do I get shit on from time to time? Most definitely. But I think that says more about the Negative Nancy's of the world than it does about me.

"Dang it, I better get going," I tell Jen as I glance down at my phone. "The next bus will be here in ten minutes."

She helps me gather my purse and resume, then hands me a pair of black heels that she insists are perfect with my outfit.

After shuffling out the door in a rush, I look behind my shoulder and see the bus fast approaching. *Dammit, I'm going to have to run to catch it.*

I hate running. My philosophy on running is that it's only necessary when being chased by a wild animal or a serial killer. I'll have to add "late for a life-changing interview" to the approved list of running activities.

The city bus doesn't even slow down as it passes me, and I make a wretched screeching noise as muddy water splashes up from the puddle on the road, soaking me from head to toe. I was in such a rush I didn't even realize it was raining. I'm frozen in place, muddy water dripping into my mouth as I stare, slack-jawed, at the rude bus driver.

My anger passes in an instant like it always does, and I'm left feeling pretty damn sorry for myself. The expensive blouse I bought for this interview is stained and soaking wet, clinging to my excessive curves.

So much for trying to find a flattering top. The pencil skirt is a bit snug, which isn't surprising, considering my wide hips, but now everyone will be able to see my muffin top.

I look back over my shoulder, mentally calculating how long it will take me to run the few blocks back home, change, and catch another bus. Too long, I decide. Especially since I already see the next city bus headed toward my stop.

Taking a deep breath, I begin wringing the water from my hair and clothes, then dry off my bus pass with a tissue from my purse. The bus stops this time, the automatic doors opening to reveal a large, middle-aged man with kind brown eyes. If he thinks it's weird to have a drowned rat on his bus, he sure doesn't show it. I suppose as long as my bus pass is charged, he could care less who paid the fare.

Once in my seat, I pull out more tissues and attempt to pat my face dry. My once neatly done chignon bun is a bird's nest of half dry, half wet, matted hair. Digging around in my purse for more bobby pins, I try my best to salvage the situation, but I think everything might fall apart with one good tug.

I know the feeling.

Sighing, I slump back in my seat and stare at the city as it passes me by. I pinch the fabric of my blouse between my thumb and pointer finger, pulling the material away from my skin and letting some air flow through. Maybe if I keep doing it, I'll be dry by the time I show up at the enigmatic Reed Landis's house.

Reed is the Dean of Fordham University, a private college here in New York. I may have googled him in preparation for this interview. If I did, it was definitely a mistake. Instead of learning anything important that might help me with my interview, I ended up scrolling through photo after photo of the giant Viking of a man. That's right. Reed is a Viking in a three-piece suit. Lord, give me strength.

He has dark hair with a sprinkling of salt and pepper on his temples. It makes him look distinguished, experienced, and worldly. A strong brow leads to a straight nose, chiseled cheekbones, and a sharp jaw, mostly covered in stubble. And his eyes. Holy Mother Earth, are they green. Greener than green. The purest green known to man, I'm sure of it.

Again, none of that is useful information for this interview. Instead, I'm more nervous than ever, knowing I look like I just wrestled a Ninja Turtle in the sewers of NYC.

My stop is announced, and I collect my things, waiting for the bus to stop before stepping off. Looking down at my phone, I see I'm already two minutes late, and I still have to hike up a hill to get to Mr. Landis's home.

I straighten my shoulders, grit my teeth, and start walking.

Crap, these heels were a mistake. I'm already accident-prone, but I'm sure I look like a baby deer trying to balance on these heels while power-walking uphill.

One foot in front of the other, I tell myself. This will be an adventure, whether I get the job or not. My parents instilled in me at an early age that the journey is just as important as the destination. They both loved extreme sports and would tell me all about their adventurous stories at night as I drifted off to sleep.

I never got into extreme sports, or any sports, for that matter. I'm sure it had something to do with the tragic skiing accident that took my mom and dad far too soon. It's still devastating, and I'll never stop loving or missing them. As the years have gone by, I've learned to appreciate their outlook on life.

Of course, I wish they were still here. I long for that every day. But I still admire my parents for taking risks, chasing dreams, and making sure they squeezed every moment from life they could. They died young, but even at thirty-two and thirty-four, I can confidently say they shared more experiences and memories than most people do at eighty.

"Ah!" I shriek, my heel catching on the uneven sidewalk. My arms pinwheel in the air, and I yank my foot forward, trying to wedge the shoe free. The heel snaps off, sending me tumbling to the ground. I land rather ungracefully but thank god I only have scrapes and bruises. It wouldn't be the first time I sprained my ankle while escaping from a high heel fiasco.

I do what I do best, and pick myself up, shake it off, and keep pressing on, broken heel or not.

Thus, I find myself hobbling up to the open front gates of the Landis estate, one shoe on my foot, one dangling from my fingers, hair a mess, clothes askew and damp, and my makeup, which I painstakingly applied with the help of YouTube, dripping down my face.

Yup, I definitely look like someone you should trust your kid with.

I'm here, though, so I might as well give it my best shot.

Raising a trembling hand to the solid oak door, I rap my knuckles against it exactly once before the door flies open. Holy hotness, I'm not prepared for this. Not the interview, and certainly not for the giant looming over me, his green eyes pinning me in place while he inhales deeply.

"Reed Landis?" I squeak out, dropping my fist from where I was knocking.

The man nods once, his lips pressed into a straight line. I can feel the warmth of his gaze traveling down my body once, then back up, up, up, until green eyes lock on mine. It takes a second for me to find my breath again. Reed is beautiful in a tragic way. Cold and untouchable and achingly lonely. I can tell that right away.

"Why do you look like that?" he grunts.

I blink a few times, then remember what a mess I am. "You will *not* believe the morning I've had," I reply, finding my footing once again. "I didn't even know it was raining until the bus splashed me as it flew by my stop! And then these shoes... let me tell you about these shoes. My roommate is going to kill me for breaking her heels, but–"

Reed turns around, giving me his back. I stop talking, not sure what he's doing. I think he's about to slam the door in my face, but he keeps walking, leaving me standing in the doorway. I guess this is all the invitation I'm going to get, so I take it.

Stepping inside, I pause briefly to take off my remaining shoe but then sprint to catch up with Reed again. His strides are so long, and he's walking so fast as if he's already frustrated with me. Not off to a good start.

"I'm so sorry I'm late." I try again, a little breathless from keeping pace with him. "I promise I'm usually more punctual."

"Sure," he mutters under his breath.

I frown, but my face softens as soon as I see the sweet little girl hiding with her blankie under a side table across from what appears to be a home office.

"Hey, sweetheart," I say softly, kneeling to get on her level.

The ad I responded to for the nanny position said the girl I'd be watching over is Kayla, and she recently lost her parents in a car accident. She was left in the care of her uncle, who is very well-off, but hasn't the faintest idea how to handle a kid. I might be filling in some of the blanks, but one look at Reed, and I know he's overwhelmed with his new lot in life.

I can feel Kayla's pain and uncertainty as she blinks up at me with round, blue eyes. She doesn't say anything at first, but that's okay. I have words enough for both of us. "I love your blanket. It looks so soft! Is pink your favorite color?"

She looks at me, then at Reed, who I notice for the first time is standing right behind me. He must have stopped his marathon to come observe me with his niece. Finally, Kayla nods her head, giving me the tiniest, shyest smile. Oh, Lord, I'm in trouble here. She's freaking adorable, and I can also tell she's got some fight in her.

"Pretty," Kayla says, pointing to my butterfly brooch.

"Do you like butterflies?"

"Butt flies?" she repeats, scrunching up her cute little nose.

I giggle, and she narrows her eyes at me. I can sense that temper right beneath the surface. One wrong word or misunderstanding and I have no doubt this little girl would rain down hell on everyone in this mansion.

I keep smiling at her, then remove the pin, making sure to close it once it's off my blouse. "Butterfly," I repeat, showing her the brooch. "Here, will you keep this safe for me while I talk to your uncle?"

"Really?" Her suspicious gaze turns into pure wonder.

"Really, really," I confirm. "It matches your beautiful necklace." Kayla reaches for the heart-shaped locket, clutching it the same way I used to clutch my mom's brooch. "Let me put it on for you." Kayla stands tall and proud as I pin the butterfly to her shirt. "Absolutely gorgeous!" Kayla beams up at me then holds out her blanket.

"Here," she says, shoving it into my hands. "You are cold and wet. My blanket will help."

I want to hug her for her kindness, but I don't know her boundaries yet. I went through phases of grief where I was annoyingly clingy, and others when I didn't want anyone to see me, let alone touch me.

"Thank you very much, Kayla. That's so thoughtful of you."

She nods and is about to say something else when Reed clears his throat.

"I have five more interviews after this," he grunts. "Hurry up." With that, he spins on his heel and stomps into the office across the hall.

"Good luck," Kayla whispers.

I smile at her, then unfold myself from the floor and follow Reed.

If nothing else, I made a sad little girl smile for half a second. That's worth all the trouble it took to get here. I just pray I can also leave with a job.

Chapter 2

Soft footsteps follow me into the study, and I quicken my pace, wanting to be further away from the too young, too innocent Josephine Clemons.

I should have shut the door on her or told her the position was already taken. I almost did, too. One look at the redhead with bright blue eyes, and I knew she couldn't possibly be the right fit.

Or maybe she's the perfect fit.

I grunt, dismissing that thought. What is wrong with me? As soon as those clear blue eyes hit mine, I felt... well, that's just it. I *felt*.

My sister, Christy, and her husband, John, died in a car accident a few months ago, and since then, I've been numb to the world. Numb to everything except taking care of my six-year-old niece, Kayla. The poor girl lost everything and ended up with me as a consolation parent. I have no idea what I'm doing, only that I'm screwing everything up.

I love my niece, but I don't know how to talk to her, how to interact. Do I bring up her parents? Or let her talk about them first? Are her temper tantrums a normal part of the grieving process, or have I somehow ruined her temperament in the nine weeks she's been with me? I don't know. I don't fucking know.

I hate not knowing things. I've made my career out of higher education as both a professor and now a dean at a private university here in New York City. When I don't have an answer to something, I do research. In this case, I've ordered thirteen books on parenting, adoption, children facing major loss, childhood grief, and anything else I thought was tangentially related to the insurmountable task of raising a child in these circumstances.

The books are currently stacked up in the corner of my bedroom, where they've remained since they were delivered. Turns out, you don't get a lot of free time with a kid on your hands, and every spare moment I have is dedicated to catching up on work and sleep.

Needless to say, I'm out of my element and failing miserably at the task my sister bestowed upon me; the care of her only child.

I reach the desk at the far end of the office and take a deep breath before exhaling heavily.

"Once again, I just wanted to apologize for being late," Josephine says, her soft voice tugging at something deep in my chest.

I rub my hand over my heart, massaging away the tight feeling there. Spinning around on my heel, I don't realize how close Josephine is. The woman is so short the top of her head doesn't even reach my shoulder.

She jerks back to avoid getting hit in the face with my elbow, then starts falling backward as her bare feet slip out from under her. Without thinking, I reach out, grabbing onto her shoulders to steady her.

Fuck.

I drop my hands immediately and shove them into my pockets for fear I'll reach out again. That one touch sent a shock wave through me, waking up a certain part of my anatomy for the first time in years. A decade? More?

Josephine is blushing, the red in her cheeks a darker shade than her fiery hair. For the first time, I notice light brown freckles dotted across her nose and cheeks. She looks so fucking adorable I can hardly breathe.

Adorable?

Shit. This isn't good. The petite woman with mouthwatering curves I'm definitely not looking at is trouble. I'm shocked when I hear myself say, "Take your seat and we'll start the interview."

I tell myself it's because she's already here, and I might as well follow through, but I keep suppressing the thought that I want to spend more time with her. I don't want to send her back out in the cold and rain. Not without a hot shower, a bowl of soup, and her phone number.

"Experience?" I growl, more forcefully than I meant. I can't let these thoughts distract me. I can't very well take care of the mess of a woman in front of me when I can't even take care of Kayla.

Once again, clear blue eyes meet mine, and Josephine gives me a shy smile, nibbling on her bottom lip. I want to wrap her up in my arms, tell her how precious she is, and also send her packing. After shutting myself off from the world for months, these conflicting emotions are overwhelming.

"Yes, well, as you can see from my resume..." she pauses, digging through her purse. A few moments later, Josephine pulls out a damp, wrinkled piece of paper with most of the ink washed out or bleeding down the page. A casualty of the rain, I assume. Josephine laughs nervously and shoves the paper back into her purse. "Sorry about that," she hedges. "I can email you a copy."

"Don't bother."

Her shoulders drop, and guilt chokes me up. What the hell? I've given stern warnings and outright anger-driven lectures to students in need of course correction, but never once have I felt guilty for my words. Now? Now, I want to punch myself in the face for making this girl sad.

"Uh, just tell me," I add against my better judgment.

Josephine pops her head up, giving me a sparkling smile. It's the same one she gave Kayla when she knelt beside her. I understand why Kayla broke her silent treatment game to talk to Josephine. I think I might do anything to get Josephine to keep smiling like that.

My niece and I had a fight over her not getting dessert yesterday, and she hasn't spoken to anyone since. I prefer the silent treatment over her outbursts of tears and screaming. I don't know how to handle either, but at least one of them comes with blessed quiet.

"I'm probably not as experienced as some of the other candidates," Josephine begins. "But I love working with kids. I used to volunteer at the Boys and Girls Club after school, running a tutoring program for elementary kids. I've had tons of experience babysitting since I grew up in several foster homes with lots of younger children and babies. And I know I'm young, but I'm dedicated and reliable. Well, except for today, what with me being late and showing up looking like the Lochness monster's regurgitated breakfast."

I lift my eyebrows in surprise and choke out a cough to cover up the sudden laughter that bubbles out of me. When was the last time I laughed? It's been a while, even before my sister's death.

Josephine is wringing her hands in her lap nervously after her rambling answer to my question. I push back the urge to cup my hands around hers and tell her she never has to be shy or embarrassed around me, but that would be crazy. Maybe I'm finally having my long-overdue mental breakdown. There's no other explanation for these tender, obsessive thoughts over a woman I met five minutes ago.

"Any experience cooking and cleaning? I'll need help around the house once I go back into the office full-time." Again, I don't know why I'm still conducting this interview. I shouldn't give her the job. And yet, I find myself on the edge of my seat - literally - to hear her answer.

"Oh. Sure, yeah, I can clean, no problem," she says a little too hesitantly to be believed. "And c-cook. Yup. If there's one thing I love, it's cooking up a storm." Josephine nods her head enthusiastically, sending a few locks of her bright red hair tumbling out of the messy bun at the base of her neck.

I watch the strands curl around her face, making her look sweet and wholesome.

I want to show her how filthy she can be. How filthy I can make her.
No, dammit!
Looking at her big blue eyes, I can tell she's not being truthful. The woman can't lie worth shit, and something about that softens me. It's

one more adorable thing about her that I can't stand. At least, that's what I'm telling myself.

"What meals do you cook?" When pink creeps up into her round cheeks, I get a twisted sense of satisfaction.

"All sorts of things," she's quick to supply. "Chicken, pizza, broccoli, bagels... um, roasts?"

"Is that a question?"

"People eat roasts. Like roast beef and stuff." She gives a firm nod, proud of herself for listing off random foods.

It should piss me off, but it doesn't. "I see."

"I can learn new recipes! You probably have a more sophisticated pallet. Um, let's see... I can make caviar, I think. That's fish eggs, right? Can you buy just the eggs, or do you have to buy the fish and cut the eggs out of their belly?" Her eyes go wide as saucers and then she covers her mouth with one hand before mumbling, "How awful. I don't think I can make caviar. I'm sorry, Mr. Landis."

I have to work extra hard not to crack a smile. Who is this woman? And why do I find her utterly irresistible and cute?

"That's okay. I've never acquired a taste for caviar."

"Whew." She exhales dramatically, dropping her hand from her mouth. "Good. Crisis averted." Josephine shines her smile on me, and I try not to feel how it warms me up and makes my stomach flip.

I'm about to ask what hours she's available to work, even though I have no intention of hiring her, when the door swings open. A distressed Kayla comes running in, and my heart stops. Her tears gut me every time, and I feel helpless to do anything about them.

Josephine is out of her chair in the next second, rushing over to Kayla. I watch in complete amazement as Kayla wraps her arms around Josephine's legs and buries her face into the side of Josephine's leg.

"Stay," the little girl cries. "Don't leave me."

"Oh, sweetheart," Josephine says soothingly, carefully untangling herself from Kayla so she can kneel next to her. "You're going to have so much fun with whoever your new nanny is. I just know they are going to love you."

Well, fuck. Josephine knows she's not getting the job, but more upsetting is that Kayla is already attached to her.

"I want *you* to be my nanny," my niece bellows.

Josephine looks at me over her shoulder, and then Kayla hits me with her watery gaze and trembling bottom lip. How can I say no to that? I'd be a monster to take away someone else from Kayla.

I'll just have to deal with these... urges. I can't touch the nanny. Can't think about the nanny. Can't fantasize about her curves or wrapping her hair around my fist while I sink into her from behind. Can't fall for her adorable quirks and sparkling eyes. No way. Not going to do any of that. Strictly professional from here on out.

"You'll start immediately," I announce. Kayla squeals in delight, and I feel like I finally did something right for once. Josephine continues to stare at me, tilting her head to the side as if trying to figure me out. "I've changed the requirements, though. It will be a live-in position."

"What?"

What?

I'm asking myself the same thing. What? Why did I say that? When did I decide the position would be live-in?

"Are you still interested?" Half of me wants her to say no, while the other half is begging, pleading with her to say yes.

"Uh..."

"Yes!" Kayla exclaims. "We can have sleepovers and play and I can show you my dolls!"

Josephine turns her attention back to Kayla, giving her a warm smile. "That sounds lovely, Kayla."

"Does that mean you'll take the job?" I ask, needing her to say the words.

"She'll take it!" Kayla answers.

Josephine laughs, the light, tinkling sound filling the room and fracturing the hard surface of my heart. "You heard the boss," she says jokingly.

"I'll send someone for your things," I inform her, busying myself with shuffling papers around on my desk. If I look at Josephine any longer, I might do something utterly insane. I might stride across the office and wrap her and Kayla up in a bear hug.

"That's not necessary. I don't have much, and the furniture and everything belongs to my roommates. I won't take up too much space with my clothes and such."

"I'll have my designer stop by tomorrow. Tell her everything you need for your room and how you'd like it to be styled."

"Oh, no, really, I'm not fussy."

I grunt, not wanting to explain my motivation. It's not that I think she's particular about her living accommodations, it's that I want her to have things she likes. I didn't miss the fact that she said she grew up in foster care. I'm sure after being a guest in lots of homes, she's learned to make do and be grateful for what she has. Under my roof, however, I'm going to give her everything her heart desires. From afar, of course. No touching. No flirting, not that I know how to do that anyway.

"She'll be here in the morning," I say with a tone of finality.

I can tell Josephine is about to push back on that, but then Kayla hops up and tugs on Josephine's arm, chattering away about giving her a tour.

"And then I can show you my reading nook. I don't read much, but I like the pictures."

"I could read some books to you," Josephine offers.

Kayla gasps and nods her head, pulling Josephine out the door. The redheaded beauty gives me one last look over her shoulder before disappearing down the hall.

I prop my elbows up on my desk and rest my head in my hands. What the hell did I just do? And how am I going to keep my distance from the curvy goddess with fiery hair and blue eyes that melt my fucking heart?

Chapter 3

Josephine

The alarm on my phone goes off, but I'm already up, scrolling through breakfast recipes on Pinterest. After a whirlwind of tours, contracts, and a sad trip to my run-down apartment to pack up my suitcases, I crashed in the guest room here at Reed's home. I guess it's my room now, but it still feels unreal.

I've never had a room all to myself. I typically shared rooms with one or two other kids growing up, though sometimes all I was given was a sleeping bag, a lumpy pillow, and the instruction to sleep wherever I could fit.

I swing my legs over my new bed and take in the grandeur of the room I'm currently staying in. The king-size bed covered in silk sheets only takes up a quarter of the space. There's a desk in one corner and a dresser in the other, as well as a walk-in closet and en-suite bathroom. If I got a hot plate and a mini-fridge, I'd be set for life.

A yawn escapes my mouth as I stretch my back and roll my shoulders. Today is the first day of my new adventure. I'm not sure what to think of Reed yet, but I already love Kalya to pieces. She's sweet, stubborn, and opinionated, that's for sure. She's also drowning in grief. Reed is, too, though I don't think he's processed any of it. I have my work cut out for me when it comes to bringing this family closer together. And it starts with a good breakfast.

If only I knew how to cook.

Sighing, I grab my phone again, looking at the three recipes I saved. I may have lied a little bit about loving to cook. Just a smidge. I'm sure I *will* love cooking. Once I figure out how to do it. I've never had the time or money to experiment with recipes, so my diet consists of microwave meals, noodles, and anything that doesn't need to be cooked - fruits, veggies, cookies, and chips. All the essential food groups.

No time like the present to learn a new skill, I think to myself. I'm nothing if not resourceful, and I'd like to think my parents would be proud of me for taking on such a challenge.

I hop off the bed with a renewed sense of purpose and slip on an oversized sweatshirt over my tank top and leggings. It hits just above my knees, covering most of my curves nicely. I found it at a thrift shop, and I adore it.

Pastel blue and pink hearts dot the fabric, along with little cartoon cats. Each cat is doing something different - one is singing, one is wearing sunglasses, another one has a cowboy hat, and so on. It's eclectic, vintage, and honestly, something no one else would probably wear. That's why I love it. Why dress like everyone else if you can wear cartoon cats instead? Seems like a no-brainer to me.

I can dress in professional clothes later. Mornings were made for baggy pajamas, in my opinion. Besides, Mr. Landis changed the rules by making it a live-in position. No way am I wearing scratchy blouses and form-fitting skirts twenty-four-seven.

I grab a scrunchie from my purse and attempt to wrestle my wild hair into a braid. After finding my lime green fuzzy slippers, I grab my phone and head out to the kitchen, ready to take on breakfast.

As quietly as I can, I open the fridge in search of eggs and milk. Next, I pull out a loaf of bread from the pantry, along with cinnamon, sugar, and vanilla extract. French toast sounds amazing, and who doesn't love dessert for breakfast? I think it's an excellent way to start my tenure here at the Landis estate. Plus, the recipe I found makes it look really simple.

I get the egg mixture ready, then read through the recipe again to make sure everything is right. The instructions say to fry the slices individually on a skillet, but that doesn't seem very efficient. Reed is a big guy. I bet he has to eat six thousand calories a day to keep up all that muscle. He'll eat five pieces easily just by himself. And Lord knows I have a sweet tooth as well. I'll be here all morning flipping toast at this rate.

But what can I use to make this process faster?

Digging around in the cupboards for a moment, a plan begins to hatch. I find a large sheet pan that can easily fit a dozen slices of bread. Perfect.

I place the pan on the counter and then stare at the oven settings, trying to figure out how to turn the dang thing on. It looks like a control board for a spaceship or a soundboard in a recording studio. Neither of which I know how to operate. No big deal. It can't be that complicated.

I hit a few buttons until a little icon with a flame lights up. That has to be a good sign. The oven beeps at me, the display flashing "350" in a bright turquoise light. If three-fifty is the default, I should turn it way up since the skillet would be hot. Right? That logic seems solid to me. I keep hitting the plus button until the screen reads five-fifty. I hit enter with a satisfied nod, then move on to the next step.

I start dipping bread into the egg mixture as the oven preheats before lining the slices up on the sheet pan. Once the pan is full, I add an extra sprinkle of cinnamon on top, proud of myself for how tasty it looks already.

"Into the oven you go," I murmur.

Wiping my hands off on my leggings, I look around at the counter. Little bits of eggshell are scattered about, plastered to the counter with dried egg residue. A fine dusting of cinnamon coats every surface, and breadcrumbs litter the floor. No problem, I'll just clean up while I wait for the French toast to cook.

I search for a rag to wipe down the counters but get distracted by a bowl of fruit in the corner next to the fridge. The bright colors of red and green apples, bananas, pears, and clementines capture my attention. This would make a perfect side for the toast!

Excitedly, I grab the basket and dump it on the counter, realizing a bit too late that wasn't the best way to get to the goods. An apple falls to the floor with a thud, rolling across the kitchen before wedging itself under the fridge. A clementine follows the path of the apple, though it's smaller, so it disappears under the fridge, never to be seen again.

I grimace as I quickly gather the remains of the fruit bowl before anything else can escape. Taking a deep breath, I regroup, searching for a cutting board and knife. I usually don't cut up my fruit, but I want this first meal I make to be pretty, and if there's one thing I know about rich people, it's that they care about appearances.

I get to work peeling and slicing the bananas, followed by a red apple, a green apple, and two pears. Arranging everything on a large tray I found in one of the cupboards, I stand back and admire my work.

"It's just missing one thing..." I whisper to myself as I reach for three clementines. I place the tiny citrus fruit in the middle of the tray, making them look like the center of a flower with fruit slices blooming all around it.

I'm so proud of my work, I grab my phone to snap a picture. Jen will never believe I did this by myself.

My thumb hovers over the screen, poised to take the snapshot when a loud, piercing siren cuts through the early morning silence.

I shriek, dropping my phone and spinning around. The oven, which I've completely neglected in my frenzy of fruit slicing, has black smoke curling up from behind and below, and I'm suddenly aware of an acrid, bitter, burnt smell in the air.

All too late, I realize I forgot to set a timer for the toast. Smoke clouds billow up, covering the room in a gray haze. The fire alarm continues to screech as I grab a dish towel and start flapping it around, trying to clear the air.

"What the hell is going on?" a powerful, harsh voice yells.

Shit.

"Mr. Landis," I exclaim, turning my head to see him step into the kitchen. "It's all under control!" I tell him cheerfully, even though I have no idea what I'm doing. "I forgot to set a timer, but don't you worry. I'll just get the toast out of the oven here..."

I open up the oven, then stumble back when thick, black smoke rolls out like a wave, covering my face and burning my eyes.

"Unbelievable," Reed mutters as he charges right for me.

I barely have time to admire his bare, chiseled chest before he wraps his arm around my waist and lifts my entire body, carrying me across the kitchen into the safety of the living room. Reed sets me down, then spins me around, giving me a once over.

"You hurt?" he grunts.

I shake my head no, my eyes never leaving his. Reed gives me a firm nod, then turns away from me, stomping back into the kitchen and hitting the cancel button on the fire alarm. I follow close behind, ready to help him clean up.

"If you just take the toast out of the oven, I'll clean the rest!" I inform Reed as I grab a clean dish towel by the sink and turn on the water, wetting it down.

"Why is there toast in the oven? We have a toaster," he grunts, pulling out the pan of charcoal toast. My face falls when I see the blackened remains of breakfast

"It's French," I say as I step out of the way. I watch Reed dump the tray into the sink, covering everything in cold water, which causes steam to hiss and fill the room.

"French," he snorts. I can't tell if he's satisfied with that answer or if he's mocking me. I choose to believe it's the former.

"Yeah. I, uh... It was my first experiment with French toast, so now I know to stick with the skillet next time."

Reed is still standing at the sink, and he tilts his head to the side as he studies me. I'm not sure what he's thinking about, and it's making me jittery inside. I break eye contact first, focusing my attention on the window above the sink.

Taking a step in that direction, I hesitate briefly, then lean over the sink, tugging the window pane up to let some fresh air in. I can't quite reach it, so I get up on my tiptoes and stretch, my left foot lifting off the ground for better leverage. My fingers graze the window, and I launch myself forward, determined to do at least one thing right this morning.

My right foot slips - it turns out fuzzy slippers don't have a lot of traction - and I scramble to right myself before falling on my ass. A large, warm hand spreads out over my back, then curls around my hip, anchoring me in place.

I peer at Reed over my shoulder, giving him a sheepish smile. Dark eyes stare back at me, equal parts frustrated and annoyed. I know that look. I used to get it a lot growing up, especially after a clumsy accident. I hate the vulnerable feeling creeping down my spine and splitting me open.

"Sorry," I mumble, stepping away from him. "Just trying to air the place out."

"Josephine..."

"Sorry about breakfast," I say, cutting him off. He can't fire me if I don't let him get a word in edgewise, right? "I'll do better. Stick to the recipes from now on. I did cut some fruit, though, so the morning wasn't a total waste," I ramble on. "Look at the time! I better go check on Kayla."

Spinning around as fast as I can without tripping, I book it down the hallway toward Kayla's room.

"Josephine," his voice booms, the tone firm and commanding.

My feet stop, and I'm frozen in place, helpless to do anything but wait for Reed's next words. I can feel the heat radiating from him as he steps up behind me. I'm too anxious to turn around, too rattled to even take a breath. My heart jumps around in my chest, each riotous beat pulsing throughout my body.

"Look at me," he says softly. It's nearly a whisper. Tears threaten to spill down my cheeks, though I'm not sure if it's from the excitement of the morning, the fear of being fired, or the surprising tenderness in Reed's voice.

I shake my head no.

"Turn around, sweetness."

Sweetness? Oh, lord, I thought my heart was racing before, but now I'm like the damn Energizer Bunny.

Slowly, I shuffle my feet and face Reed, though I can't look him in the eye. He surprises me further by gently gripping my chin between his thumb and forefinger, tipping my head up.

I'm expecting to see anger, disappointment, or indifference as if he's already mentally moved on to the next nanny. Instead, dark eyes lock onto mine, and I'm overwhelmed by the concern swimming in their depths. His brow furrows as he drops his hand from my chin, only to cup the side of my face.

I inhale sharply, the unexpected contact lighting me up and making me feel all sorts of confusing things. My stomach flips, and a warm, tingling sensation crawls down my spine, landing right between my thighs.

Reed swipes his thumb over my cheek, catching a tear and wiping it away. "You lied," he grunts.

I'm jarred out of whatever spell he had me under, and I take a step back. Of course, he's upset. He knows I lied about being able to cook, and now he's going to really let me have it.

"I can learn how to cook, okay?" I say with more defensiveness than I meant. "I'll start with an easier meal next time. No international cuisine until I've mastered the classics."

I swear Reed's lip twitches up in one corner, and for one brief, brilliant moment, I think he's going to smile. But then he schools his expression, giving me his now-familiar stern gaze.

"I meant about being hurt. You're crying."

"Oh." *What?* This man is confusing, and he's getting me all twisted up inside. "No, I'm not hurt. I'm... It's..." I look down at the floor, noticing for the first time that Reed is barefoot. I don't know why that fact makes me smile, but it does. "I'm fine," I finally land on.

"Jo–"

"What smells?" Kayla shouts as she clambers down the stairs.

"You can get her ready for the day while I clean and go for breakfast, take two?" I ask Reed, taking a few more steps back.

His hand lingers in the air like he was about to pull me closer, but then he drops it. Clearing his throat, Reed runs a hand through his hair, then looks behind him at the disaster zone. I really did make a mess.

"You take Kayla. I'll deal with breakfast."

"Are you sure?"

"Wouldn't want to risk burning the kitchen down for a second time in your first few hours on the clock, would you?"

My jaw drops when he smirks at me.

Holy freaking balls, he's devastating. Gorgeous. Playful. Bright and sparkling.

And then the light from his eyes is gone, the same reserved, grumpy Reed back at the helm.

I decide not to try my luck at defying him just yet, though he'll need to start interacting with Kayla at some point. I'm hoping to facilitate a conversation or two over breakfast.

"You win this time," I tell him as I head toward Kayla's room.

"By the way, we usually have cereal for breakfast. In case you were wondering, it doesn't require the oven."

I snort out a laugh, but I don't dare look back at him. If I see that sexy smirk one more time, I might do something stupid, like throw myself into his arms and beg him to give me my first kiss.

No, I need to focus on my mission. Helping Kayla and Reed connect. Not *me* and Reed. Right. Just need to keep that straight, and I'll be fine. Everything will be fine.

Chapter 4

My phone buzzes, pulling me away from the five-hundred-page budget proposal for the History department. I've been reading the document all morning, but I've only gotten through the first twenty pages.

Fuck, my brain isn't used to this much concentrated work time after the last few months. I used to power through department finances and streamline most requests, but I've barely worked twenty hours a week while figuring things out with Kayla.

Another rattling vibration from my phone throws off my focus completely, and I curse as I snatch it off the desk.

"What?" I mutter into the phone, not even looking to see who it is.

"Happy Saturday to you, too," Emmaline, my youngest sister, replies.

"Em." I try again with less frustration in my voice. She's a good kid, just turned twenty-one, and is still figuring out life away from our toxic mother. "I wasn't expecting your call."

"Are you ever?" she teases. "I just wanted to check-in and see how the new nanny is working out. I know it was a hard decision to make."

I sigh and lean back in my chair, feeling a lead weight settling on my chest. It's true. I was resistant to hiring anyone to help with Kayla. Christy and her husband, John, entrusted me with the care of their daughter. No way in hell was I going to outsource the most important job I've ever been given.

I severely underestimated how much work parenthood is, however. Add on a grieving little girl with mood swings and a scream fit for a banshee, and yeah, I can admit when I'm out of my depth. As much as I hate it, I understand that I have limits.

"The nanny," I repeat, shooing away images of Josephine's blue eyes and pink cheeks. She's been here for almost a week now, and I still can hardly look at her without my chest growing tight... and my pants. Jesus, I'm a mess.

"Did you fire her already?" Emmaline asks, bringing me back into the moment.

I clear my throat and rub my eyes, pushing back the inappropriate thoughts. "No, I didn't fire her."

"But you're going to?"

"What makes you say that?"

"You're not exactly..." she trails off, searching for the right word. "You can be a little stuck in your ways," she finally hedges.

"Having a routine isn't the same as being stuck in my ways," I grumble.

"I mean, it kind of is," Emmaline teases. "Besides, you didn't answer my question. How are things going?" I'm about to answer when she cuts me off. "And don't say *fine*. Things are not fine, Reed, and that's okay."

I grunt, not liking how well she knows me despite our eighteen-year age gap. Emmaline wasn't a planned pregnancy for our mother. Technically, she's a half-sister to Christy and me, but that doesn't matter. Family is family.

When she was born, I had already moved to New York with a childhood friend, Dylan, who still works with me as a professor. Christy was a junior in high school at the time, and I know she was just as eager to get away from our dysfunctional home and addict mother as I was.

"It's been an adjustment," I say, thinking back on the week. "She almost burned down the damn kitchen the first morning she was here. Can't cook to save her life. We've been surviving on takeout and pasta. I don't think she's taken the garbage out once. Honestly, the place is messier since she started working for me."

Even though it's true, I get a bitter taste in my mouth with each disparaging word I say about Josephine. I can't stop thinking about the morning of the fire, and not because of the alarm, the smoke, or the awful stench that stuck around the kitchen for a few days.

It was her. Josephine. When she stumbled away from me, I felt my heart plummet to the ground. I called out her name, and she stopped in her tracks as if waiting for my next command. My anger splintered apart when she turned around, leaving an aching need to protect the redheaded beauty. I shouldn't have touched her. Shouldn't have wiped away her tears or cupped her face. Now I know how soft she is, how precious. And I can't do a damn thing about it.

"Right?" Emmaline asks. I realize she's been talking up a storm, and I haven't been paying attention to a single word.

"Yep," I'm quick to answer.

Em snorts a laugh, and I feel my lips pulling to the side. It's not quite a smile, but it's more than I've done in a long time. "You have no idea what I just said, do you?"

"How is your new job? Are you still liking California? Couldn't have picked a state further away from me, huh?"

Emmaline doesn't answer at first, but then she takes mercy on me and lets me change the subject, filling me in on her coworkers and studio apartment. I nod and ask questions here and there, wanting her to know she still has family who cares.

I have a lot of regrets in life, but not being there for Emmaline during her childhood is perhaps my biggest one. I visited a few times, but it was difficult being home. Christy spent more time with her over the years, but Em and I have always shared letters and phone calls. I can't be the kind of friend and confidant Christy was, but I'm trying. In the end, though, I just feel like it's one more way I'm failing everyone in my life. I can't be what Christy was.

"So, anyway," Emmaline continues. "I think some of the girls from the office are finally warming up to me. They offered to take me out for drinks next weekend!"

The protective big brother in me snaps to attention. Never too late to make up for lost time. "Who? How many? Where?"

"Chill out," she laughs. "It's just a handful of us from the office. I was starting to think no one liked me, but this could be a turning point. It'd be nice to have some friends."

I grunt, knowing Emmaline is responsible and she'll be fine hanging out with some coworkers at a bar, but still not liking the fact that I won't be there. "Go to On the Rocks," I tell her. "Theo works there, you know. He'll watch out for you."

"Theo?" Emmaline's voice is strange and squeaky, and then she chokes out a cough.

"Everything okay? I told you Theo lives in Redwood, right? That's half the reason I let you move across the country, knowing my old friend would be there if you needed anything."

"*Let me*?" Emmaline counters, clearly over whatever coughing fit she was having.

I chuckle, the sound gruff and unfamiliar. "I know, I know. You're a strong independent woman who can do whatever you want in life."

"That's what I thought you said," she answers with her signature sass.

My office door cracks open, and Josephine pops her head in, those big blue eyes darting around the room until they land on mine. My dick twitches, and I clench my fist around my phone, every muscle in my body strung tight with just one look from the tempting nanny.

I nod at Josephine, silently telling her she can come in. The door swings open, banging against the wall. Josephine cringes, then steps inside the room gingerly, as if she could erase the noise with soft steps.

"Sorry to interrupt," she whispers.

I put one finger up, signaling for her to wait a minute. She nods and proceeds to walk around the perimeter of my office, getting her fingerprints on everything. I can see a smudge on the glass of one of my favorite photos from where she touched it. That should annoy me.

Instead, I want to gather her hands up in mine and kiss each of her fingers.

Fuck.

"You sound busy," Emmaline states. "Is it the new nanny? Give her some more time, Reed. Go easy on her."

"I'm not a monster," I inform my sister.

"No, just a big growly grizzly bear."

I sigh while Emmaline laughs. She says she'll call back later, and we say our goodbyes. Just in time for Josephine to stub her toe on my seven-thousand-dollar Italian leather lounge seat.

"Ouch," she mutters to herself, hopping on one foot.

I'm out of my seat the next second, needing to be near her, to comfort her or some shit. Josephine spins around, her bright red hair fanning out and glittering in the sunlight streaming through the open window. I can't breathe for a second, too mesmerized by her sparkling beauty to do anything other than stare.

And then she stumbles off-balance, lurching forward.

I gather her up into my arms, holding her close. Too close. Not close enough.

I can't bring myself to loosen my hold on this enchanting creature. Instead, I dip my head down, nuzzling into her wild hair, breathing in her strawberry scent.

"Um, Mr. Landis?" she mumbles softly, her voice muffled from where she's tucked into my chest.

I immediately drop my arms from around her waist and step back, steadying her with my hands on her shoulders.

"Yes, Josephine." I address her in the cool, detached tone I've come to perfect over my years as an educator and a dean. I've never needed it more than in my interactions with this woman.

"Sorry about that," she says, straightening her shirt and combing her fingers through her hair. "You'd think I'd see a freaking chair enough not to trip over it."

Josephine rolls her eyes at her clumsiness, but I can tell she's embarrassed. Has she had to apologize for that a lot in her life? Were her foster families mean about it? Did the other kids make fun of her for her accident-prone tendencies? All questions I'd like to know the answers to, but never will. It's not my place.

"What do you need?" I ask instead.

"I was hoping you might come outside with us."

I blink at her, confusion settling over me. "Do you need me for something? I had a top-of-the-line playground installed in the backyard that should be ready to go. I have the number for customer service if something is broken. Let me grab it."

I turn back to my desk, ready to go through the drawers to find that damn number. I paid a small fortune for the playground, and the company assured me they would respond to repairs quickly.

"No, the playground is wonderful. Kayla loves it."

"Okay. Right then. Does she want something else? A sandbox or bouncy castle or something? I probably can't get those today, but by next weekend, maybe..."

"Mr. Landis–"

"Reed," I correct for the hundredth time this week. I don't know why I insist she calls me by my first name. It definitely doesn't have anything to do with how it sounds falling off her tongue.

"Reed. What I'm trying to say is... Kayla enjoys the playground a lot. But maybe she would like to enjoy it with *you*?"

I'm still not understanding. "Is there a reason you are unable to go outside? Are you unwell? Do you need the day off?" The thought twists my stomach. Why didn't I know Josephine was sick?

"No," Josephine sighs. "I'm fine. I guess I'm asking if you'd come play with Kayla. It's Saturday, and you've been busy at the office from sun up to sun down this week. Maybe an hour with Kayla will be good for both of you?"

"I don't have time," comes my automatic response. It's true. I'm weeks behind on work. This history budget was supposed to be approved ages ago, and I have a dozen projects that need my signature before they can begin.

Not to mention, if I spend any more time with Josephine, I might slip. I might tell her how beautiful she is, how her blue eyes follow me into sleep and fill my dreams. I might count each of her freckles, then kiss them, wanting to taste every single inch of her.

"I know you have an important and demanding job, Mr. La–um, Reed. But if you could put aside an hour to come push Kayla on the swing, I promise it'll be worth it. You two need to spend some time together just having fun."

"Fun," I repeat.

Josephine nods her head, those pouty lips curling into a radiant smile. "Yeah. Just for an hour. Then you can come back here and be Serious Mr. McEducator Man."

This startles a laugh right out of me, and Josephine blushes the prettiest pink. "Serious Mr. McEducator Man?" I repeat, a grin threatening to break free.

She shrugs, looking down at her feet. They are bare, and I can see her cute little toenails painted purple. She wiggles them, and I resist the urge to kneel and kiss each one.

Stop being a psycho, I reprimand myself. No use. I still want to worship the ground her perfectly purple toes have stepped on.

"Okay," I finally say.

"Really?" The woman beams up at me, her smile hitting me with such force I have to return it. Josephine blushes again, a deeper red, then claps her hands. "Wonderful. I'll get Kayla dressed to play outside, and you can meet us down there in a few minutes. This will be good, Mr..." I lift an eyebrow, silently correcting her. "McEducator Man," she finishes with a giggle.

Goddamn, I want to bottle that sound up and carry it with me everywhere.

I watch the curvy goddess dance out of my office and wipe a hand down my face. It hasn't even been a week, and I can't seem to say no to her. My sister told me to give it more time, but I'm afraid the longer Josephine is in our lives, the less likely I am to let her go at all.

Grunting, I make my way to my bedroom to throw on some old jeans, giving myself a pep talk the entire time. I can't fuck this up for Kayla. If I started something with Josephine–who is nearly twenty years my junior and too sweet to be stuck with a grump like me–and it ended poorly... Kayla would be the one to suffer. That's not fair to her.

After waiting a few minutes to gather my thoughts, I head outside to join my niece and the redheaded beauty I can't get out of my mind.

Kayla and Josephine are sitting in front of the swingset portion of the playground, pulling the grass out. I frown as I step closer, wondering if there's something wrong with it.

"Uncle Reed!" Kayla exclaims, looking up at me with big green eyes.

Jesus, she looks like her mother. A band of pressure squeezes around my chest, pain clawing at my insides when I think about how Christy will never see her daughter grow up.

The light in her eyes dims, and I realize I must be scowling. I don't mean to. God, I'd rather get attacked by a bear than cause this little girl any more sadness. I need to keep my emotions in check around Kayla. She can't see me falling apart right now. She needs me to be strong. Everyone needs me to be strong.

Josephine hops up, holding her hand out for Kayla to take. "We're glad you're here," she says, giving me a warm smile. "Aren't we, Kayla?"

My niece nods but doesn't say anything or move an inch toward me. What am I supposed to do? Crouch down and talk about... what? I don't think Kayla has any ideas about expanding collegiate budgets or filing for tax exemptions.

I look around, hoping for something to inspire conversation in me. "What's wrong with the grass?" I blurt out when my eyes land on the patch of land the two girls were picking at.

"Um... what?" Kayla asks, following my line of sight.

"Kayla made you something," Josephine mercifully interrupts.

I look over at her and watch as she whispers something to Kayla. My niece shakes her head no but then finally holds her hand out. A few dandelions are woven together in the palm of her tiny hand.

"I'll have to call about spraying for weeds again," I say, picking up the dandelions and inspecting them.

Kayla gasps, and Josephine clears her throat. I glance at her, and she widens her eyes, trying to convey a message. "Well, good thing those are *flowers* and not weeds. *Right*?" She glares at me and then at the dandelion ring. "I think your *flower wreath* is beautiful. In fact, I'm jealous."

I've never considered myself a stupid man, but I'm feeling like an idiot right about now. "Flowers," I repeat. "Wreath. Beautiful." *Jesus, I'm a moron.*

"See? He's speechless!" Josephine grins down at Kayla, who is still skeptical of me.

"Put it on," Kayla says, crossing her arms over her chest.

I dart my eyes to Josephine, who subtly points to the top of my head. She smiles triumphantly as I place the weeds–I mean, *flowers* on my head. Kayla narrows her eyes at me, then bursts into laughter.

Thank fucking god.

"Swings!" Kayla shouts, spinning away from me and running to the swingset.

"Why do I feel like that was a test?" I ask Josephine as we follow Kayla.

"It was," she says with a grin. "Well, more like a pop quiz."

I chuckle, wanting to pull her into my arms. "And I passed?"

"With flying colors."

"Whew," I say, wiping my forehead dramatically.

Josephine laughs and bumps her shoulder with mine. She's so short, her shoulder only comes up a few inches above my elbow, but I love that she initiated contact. I get a whiff of her sweet strawberry scent, and my mouth waters. I want to know if her lips taste just as sweet.

"Ready for your next one?" Josephine nods toward the swing where Kayla is struggling to sit.

"Nope," I tell her truthfully before helping Kayla get adjusted. "Need a push?" I ask my niece.

"Yes! High, high, high, all the way to the sky!"

I grip the sides of the swing and walk backward a few steps before letting go.

"Higher!" she yells.

I push the swing gently when it comes back to me, but Kayla yells again, more frustrated this time.

"No, higher! Underdog! Underdog!"

I don't know what that is, but I push a little harder when the swing comes back again. Not much. I don't know how high is too high. What if the swing wraps around the top beam? Is that possible? I should have done more research before buying this thing. Suddenly, all I see are the dangers it presents.

Kayla lets out a frustrated growl and leaps off the swing, giving me a goddamn heart attack. She's only two and a half feet off the ground at most, but still. She's so tiny and fragile.

She lands on her feet with no problem, and I realize I may have been a little too cautious. Can she blame me? I'm just trying to protect her.

I rush over to Kayla, but she gives me a sour look before bursting into tears and running toward the slide. I watch her crawl underneath and curl up into a ball. Shit. What did I do wrong? How do I fix it? Will this parenting thing ever get any easier?

"Let me talk to her," Josephine says, resting a hand on my arm. I look down at our connection, wanting so much more but also confused as fuck about what just happened.

"I didn't want her to get hurt," I mutter, looking like even more of an idiot in front of Josephine. Why can't I do anything right?

"I know. She's not really upset with you."

I'm about to ask Josephine what the hell she means, but she's already crouching down in front of the slide. I stand back, feeling frustrated and helpless. One step forward, ten giant steps back, I guess.

"Did your mommy used to push you on the swing?" Josephine asks in a soft, calming voice.

"Yeah," comes Kayla's teary response. My gut sinks and I rub my temples. I don't know where the landmines are for this little girl, much less what to do when I accidentally step on one. "She gave me underdogs and we would sing *high, high, high, all the way to the sky.*"

I swallow thickly, picturing what a good mother Christy was. It came so naturally for her. She had intuition and grace and a silly side I never understood. I can't be that for Kayla, and it kills me.

"I love that," Josephine murmurs. "Sounds like you had a lot of fun together."

More sniffles and muffled words are exchanged, then Josephine sits down on the grass, holding her arms out. Slowly, Kayla uncurls herself from under the slide and crawls into Josephine's lap.

"You know," Josephine says softly, wiping tears from Kayla's cheeks and tucking her hair behind her ear. "I lost my parents when I was your age."

Everything in me stills and then tightens. I take a ragged breath, forcing myself to stand right here instead of scooping both her and Kayla up in my arms. I knew Josephine grew up in foster care, but I had no idea her story was so close to Kayla's.

Fuck, am I tearing up?

I tilt my head back, looking at the sky and willing my emotions to stay dormant just a little longer.

"Really?" Kalya asks.

I strain to hear the response, hanging on Josephine's every word.

"Really. I remember the first few months after they passed away, everything hurt." Kayla nods her head, then rests it on Josephine's shoulder, absentmindedly playing with her red hair. "And sometimes, I would get so angry, I felt like I couldn't contain it. I had to yell or sometimes throw things. I didn't mean to upset anyone, and I know you don't mean to upset anyone either."

"Did you live with your uncle?"

"No, I wasn't lucky enough to have any family members close by. But you have an uncle who loves you and wants good things for you. He might not get it right every time, but that just means he needs our help."

"Help? *Him?*" My niece scrunches up her nose, and I can't help but smile. She's adorable, even when she's giving me shit.

"Yeah. I think he needs a lot of it, don't you?"

"What do you mean?"

"He didn't even know what an underdog was."

The two erupt in giggles, and I take a breath for the first time in ten minutes.

Kayla wraps her arms around her nanny in a tight hug. I can see Josephine close her eyes and breathe deeply, a slight crease in her brow. Sunlight pours over her, making her hair glitter and highlighting her soft features, giving her an ethereal look.

Her eyes open, her blue irises hitting me square in the chest. A single tear forms and falls as she stares at me, squeezing Kayla in a hug. This moment is so pure, so fragile, I don't even want to breathe for fear of breaking it.

This woman is incredible. Magical. Brilliant and beautiful, and so damn vulnerable. I was afraid to share my grief with Kayla, worried it would be too much for her to handle. I see now that she was missing that human connection. Josephine hardly knows us yet, but she was willing to go to that painful place in her life if it meant comforting the little girl in her arms.

I'm in awe of Josephine. I also feel completely inadequate. I don't know if I can be vulnerable right now. Or ever.

"Should we show him how it's done?" Josephine asks.

Kayla scrambles off her lap and darts toward me, grabbing my hand as if nothing happened. Josephine stands and joins us as we walk back to the swings. I reach out for her hand, folding it in my much larger one. She looks at our twined fingers then up at me, those clear eyes full of questions. Fuck if I know any of the answers, but it feels right.

Josephine blinks a few times, her rosy cheeks turning pink as she smiles. Her freckles stand out when she blushes, and I hold myself back from tugging her closer and kissing each one.

The three of us march toward the swings, and I don't know if I've ever felt more at peace with my life. This can't last forever, but I'll cherish this moment as long as it lasts. I have to keep my distance. Stay strong.

The more I tell myself that, the less I remember why.

Shit. Am I already in too deep?

Chapter 5

"Jo Jo, what are you painting?" Kayla asks, giggling as she waves her paintbrush in the air.

I smile at her nickname for me, then spin around to face the cutest little girl I've ever seen. Her green eyes shine up at me, full of joy and wonder. It fills me with warmth to see her enjoying herself.

We've had a few rough days this last week, but there have also been moments of happiness and growth. I'll take all the wins I can get right now when it comes to Kayla and her enigmatic uncle, Reed.

"It's a hippo in a tutu!" I sing-song, adding a few more strokes of hot pink paint to my masterpiece.

Kayla laughs, telling me I need to work on my skills. I agree with her and then turn up the radio, dancing along to beat. The spirited little six-year-old wiggles her hips right along with me, her paintbrush flying over her canvas as she sings off-key.

It's Saturday again, and today Reed is upstairs working in his office. We agreed he could work Saturdays only and reserve every Sunday for Kayla time, or he could work every other weekend. I expected him to push back on this, but after seeing the improvement with Kayla after the swingset fiasco, he agreed more time together was a good thing.

Last night, Reed took Kayla out to the movies, giving me the evening off. I won't lie, I was a little disappointed I didn't get an invite to the movies. I've never had a family, and as crazy as it is, it feels like I just might fit in with this one. However, that's a dangerous thing to think, so I decided to hang out with Jen instead of letting my unrequited, confusing crush on Reed continue to fester.

I hadn't seen Jen since I moved out two weeks ago, so it was good to catch up. She and Ashley found a third roommate, who seems to be a good balance for them. I felt bad leaving my friend alone with

Ashley, but Reed offered to cover the entirety of the rent until they found someone to take my spot. I'm glad it worked out.

Still, my heart wasn't in the conversation at all, and by the end, Jen could tell I was phoning it in. I blamed it on being exhausted from my new job, but I'm not sure she bought it. At least she didn't press the issue. I've never been a very talented liar, and I don't know what I would say if she questioned me about my new boss.

After a restless night of sleep, I got up relatively early and made waffles - the microwave kind. Reed's still leery of me using the oven, and I can't blame him. Reed had to get some work done when breakfast was all cleaned up. I decided Kayla and I would go on a little walk around the property since it's so huge, then settle in for a craft day. I found some neon glitter paint that I knew Kayla was going to love.

I was right. I set up a little art studio for us in the dining room, and we've been here most of the morning, dancing, painting, and loving life. The only thing that would make it more perfect is if Reed were here.

Floorboards creak above our heads, and as if the universe heard my request, Reed stomps down the stairs. I'd say my belly is filled with butterflies, but that's much too graceful an image for what's really happening. It's more like a colony of drunken bats has taken flight, making my stomach twist and my heart thrash against my chest.

And let's not talk about what's going on with other, lower parts of me. My thighs squeeze together instinctively, my inner muscles clenching around nothing. I've never felt so achy, so *empty* around another person before. It's driving me crazy, and I have no idea what to do about it.

I can hear Reed walking through the kitchen, and I brace myself for him to step into the dining room. Looking over at Kayla, I smile when I see she's happily painting away, lime green paint in her hair and neon blue streaked across her left cheek. She's so freaking cute.

"What the hell is going on in here?" Reed growls.

Kayla's shoulders drop and she darts her eyes to me, not wanting to look at her uncle. What is his problem now? I thought we made some big steps last weekend with Kayla, and here he is, being a grumpy asshole again.

"We're painting," I say cheerfully, giving Kayla a wink. She grins at me, and my heart melts all over again. "Kayla is quite the artist."

I glance up at Reed, who is standing on the edge of the dining room with his arms crossed over his massive chest. Dark eyebrows scrunch into a frown as green eyes narrow in on me.

"The carpet is ruined," he grits out.

I furrow my brow in confusion, then look at the floor. Wincing, I notice big globs of blue and pink paint on the white carpet beneath Kayla, along with multi-colored splatters surrounding my paint station.

"Oops," I whisper, scrunching up my nose. "It's washable paint," I rush to say. "And look, I remembered to put towels down on the table." I lift one of the towels, proud of myself for thinking that far ahead. Apparently, it wasn't good enough.

"But the carpet..." Reed trails off, then sighs, rubbing a hand down his face. He looks exhausted. I want to rub the tension from his shoulders and scold him for being such a party pooper.

"It's washable," I say again, hoping he'll hear it this time. "Look, it says so right on the bottle."

Reed grabs the nearest bottle, grimacing when some pink paint gets on his hands. "Washable from *clothes*, not carpets," he mutters, leveling a look at me.

I have no idea what crawled up his ass and died, but he has no right to take out his frustration and exhaustion on us, especially Kayla.

"I'm sure I can figure out a way to get it out of the carpet. That's what YouTube was made for, right? Cleaning tips? Well, that, and cat videos. Obviously."

Kayla laughs, and I give her a little grin. We've watched dozens of cute kitty video clips this week. Reed, however, isn't satisfied with my solution.

"Just... just clean up what you can and I'll hire someone else to take care of the carpet," he grumbles. "Try not to get the paint on anything else. The furniture is antique, you know. Can't be replaced or cleaned up with a hacky internet video."

Well, that's just rude.

Kayla chooses this moment to have a meltdown. Looks like everyone in the Landis household needs a time out.

"Stop it!" Kayla screams, throwing her paintbrush at Reed.

He startles at the decibel of her screech, then glares at me as if I'm supposed to shut her up. Yeah, no chance, buddy. Should have thought of that before being a grumpy-butt.

"Stop being mean to Jo Jo!"

Reed's eyes go wide as saucers, an honest-to-god shiver running down his spine at the force behind her words. It's all I can do not to smirk. "I'm not–"

"I love my Jo Jo," Kayla continues. "But I hate you. I *hate* you!"

Shit. That escalated quickly.

I reach out for Kayla, but she pushes me away, running upstairs. Her bedroom door slams shut a few seconds later, and a heart-wrenching sob echoes through the house.

"Fuck," Reed murmurs. I look over at him as he plops down on a dining room chair, his head in his hands. He looks broken. I may be pissed at him and his bad attitude, but I hate seeing him like this.

Taking a deep breath, I wipe my hands on a towel and walk over to where Reed is sitting. "Hey," I say softly, resting my hand on his shoulder. Reed tenses, and I almost snatch my hand away, but then he relaxes under my touch, even leaning closer to me. "I'm truly sorry about the carpet. I didn't think to cover it up, but I will next time."

Reed grunts and shrugs his shoulders, never lifting his head from his hands.

I roll my eyes and take the seat next to his. "This is the part where you apologize for being a growly jerk."

I get a half-hearted laugh, which I consider a win.

"I don't know what happened while you were working in your office, but you came down here with all that negative energy, and, well, see how it turned out?"

"My negative energy didn't have anything to do with paint on the carpet."

"No, but it certainly affected your reaction to it."

Reed's shoulders drop, and he finally lifts his head. God, those green eyes bore into mine, and for one fleeting moment, he lets me see everything. His grief, his weariness, all the doubts, insecurities, and pain he's been carrying around for months, if not years. I want to crawl into his lap and wrap myself around him. I want to share his burden, learn his secrets, and heal the wounds deep in his soul.

"I don't know what the fuck I'm doing," he confesses. His voice is no more than a raspy whisper. "I'm sorry," he adds before breaking eye contact.

My hand wraps around his before I can think better of it. "I forgive you." Reed stares at our interlaced fingers for a second, then drags his eyes back up to meet mine. "See? That wasn't so hard," I say, giving him a small smile.

"I don't think Kayla will be so understanding," he says miserably. "You heard her. She hates me."

"She doesn't hate you. She's just having a lot of big emotions, and she has no idea how to express them."

Reed mumbles something that sounds like *her and me both*, but I'm not sure what that means.

"Plus," I continue, "kids say stuff they don't mean all the time. They're little balls of energy and chaos with a million thoughts floating around and no filter. Kayla even more so with her entire life being uprooted. You just need to toughen up."

Reed surprises me with a chuckle. "I don't think anyone has ever told me to toughen up."

I grin, tipping my chin up as I stare into his endless green eyes. "First time for everything then."

His gaze turns more serious, those emerald irises refusing to look away. "I suppose so," he murmurs. I'm not sure what we're even talking about anymore, but I never want this moment to end.

Reed clears his throat, leaning away from me and pulling his hand from mine. A chill sweeps through me, making me shiver at the loss of contact. I feel almost drugged as he stands up and walks to the other side of the table, busying himself with the paint supplies.

What the heck just happened?

"Reed?"

"I'll clean up," he clips out, the temperature in the room dropping at his cold tone. "I'll talk to Kayla after she calms down."

"Is everything okay?" I ask, standing up.

"It's fine. Need to clean this mess up before the stains set in for good."

This man. He's vulnerable and repentant one minute, then detached and aloof the next. He's as infuriating as he is heartbreaking, and I have no idea how to navigate these waters.

"I can help," I offer, taking a step closer.

"You've done enough."

I stop mid-step and stare at his back. I know he's hiding something, some secret pain, some perceived inadequacy. But he's too damn stubborn to let me in. Instead, Reed wants to push me away, push Kayla away.

Well, screw him, then.

"Have fun," I say sarcastically, hoping he doesn't hear the hurt in my voice. After last weekend, I thought we shared a moment, maybe even two. But here we are, back to grunts and grimaces.

Walking from the dining room, I take a second to catch my breath at the base of the stairs before heading up to check on Kayla. What am I going to do with these two?

I knock on Kayla's door, entering when I hear a sniffle. "Hey, honey," I say, sitting on the edge of her bed. All I can see is a Kayla-sized lump under the covers. "Want to talk about it?"

She sighs and lets out the cutest little growl, making me hold back a laugh. She must get it from Reed. A second later, the covers come off, and Kayla sits up, giving me a pout.

"He was being a jerk," she states. "And he was mean to you!"

I nod, letting her vent a little more. "Yes, your uncle was rude, but do you think you handled that situation well?"

Kayla glares at me, then rolls her eyes. "Yeah," she says defiantly.

"Really? I don't think it's ever appropriate to tell someone you hate them. Isn't that worse than what Reed did?"

"But... but..." Kayla sighs and flops back on her bed. She's going to be a fun teenager, I can tell. "I didn't mean it."

"I know that. But our words matter, don't you think?"

She reluctantly nods. "They do. My mom used to say that, too."

"Oh, sweetheart," I whisper, taking her little hand in mine. "I wish I could have met her."

Kayla reaches for the golden locket she always has around her neck. She hasn't shown me what's inside yet, but I have a feeling it's a photo of her parents.

"Oh, no," she squeaks. Kayla stretches out the collar of her shirt and looks down, then tips her head up, meeting my eyes with a watery gaze. "It's gone," she cries, tears spilling down her cheeks. "My necklace! My necklace!"

Oh, lord. It seems I went from the frying pan downstairs, straight into the fire upstairs. "Shh, Kayla, we'll find your necklace. I'll help you look."

The little girl cries harder, twisting her hands into fists and pounding them on her pillow. "It's outside!" she yells. "I had it this morning when we went on our walk."

Dammit. She's right. That's the last time I saw her wear it as well. I had a brilliant idea to walk around the property since Reed paid someone a truckload of money to have it landscaped. I didn't realize how far back it went either. Crap, it could be anywhere. We walked all over the place.

"I have to get it. I have to find it. Right *now*!"

Kayla leaps off the bed, but I catch her and bring her back to my side. "Hold on there, missy. We can go searching for your necklace later. I need you to stay up here until Reed comes in to talk to you. Both of you have some apologizing to do, right?" I lift an eyebrow, and Kayla sighs, nodding her head. She's a good kid. She just needs some boundaries and to be secure in her surroundings.

"But it's supposed to storm tonight," she whispers.

Double dammit. She's right again. The locket will be a lot harder to find after a storm.

"I'll tell you what. You stay here and wait for your uncle, and I'll go outside and find your necklace, okay?"

"Really?" Kayla looks up at me with such hope in her eyes. She's a sweetheart. When she's not having a temper tantrum, that is.

"Yes."

"You promise? You won't come back until you have it?"

I laugh, scooping her up in my arms. "Trying to get rid of me?"

"No! Never!" she squeals as I spin her around.

"Good." I set Kayla down on her bed and kiss the top of her head. "Your uncle loves you, Kayla. This is all new to him, too."

She nods and wraps her arms around me. I give her a squeeze then head to my room to find some shoes suitable for trudging around in the mud.

I sneak downstairs, peeking into the dining room, where Reed is scrubbing the carpet. At least he looks miserable.

Slipping out the back door, I barely make it one step into the yard before the skies open up, drenching me in two seconds flat.

Wonderful.

Chapter 6

Reed

I'm a fucking idiot.

That fact has never been more apparent than right now, as I stretch out on the dining room carpet and stare at the ceiling, exhausted from scrubbing paint for the last two hours. Kayla has her way of throwing a temper tantrum, and I have mine.

I pissed off the two most important people in my life all in one go, and I have no one to blame but myself.

Josephine was right when she called me out on my bad mood. My closest friend, Dylan, informed me he was in love with one of his students. Not only that, but he's stepping down as the professor for all of the intro to psychology courses to avoid a conflict of interest.

Dylan said he lined up one of his best doctoral students and a trusted adjunct professor to take over his course load, but it's not that simple. I almost bit his head off over the phone, but then he started talking about Sarah, and I knew his decision was final. I've never heard him quite like that before.

I'm happy for him, but that doesn't mean I can't be pissed and frustrated. I know he thinks he squared everything away, but there are always more behind-the-scenes things going on than most professors know about.

Not only did I have to work out payroll and HR things, but I had to go over the course material and double-check the schedules. Normally, it wouldn't be that big of a deal, but these classes... Fuck. These were the classes Christy taught.

She loved psychology and she had endless patience for students. I used to tease her about following in my footsteps by applying to Fordham University, and she would say I needed someone to look out for me.

I thought I was done with the flashbacks of Christy when I handed all of her classes over to Dylan. He was less than thrilled to be teaching 101 classes again. I know if anyone else would have asked him for that kind of favor, he would have said hell no, but we have history.

After dealing with painful memories and the human resources department for the entire morning, all I wanted was some peace and quiet for the afternoon. Instead, I walked in on annoying pop music blaring and paint splattered all over my carpet.

I could hear myself being unreasonable. Rude. A jerk, like Josephine said. And then Kayla said she hated me...

"Oomph," I grunt, rubbing the tightness from my chest at the memory. It *hurts*.

But could I stop myself at alienating just one person? Oh, no. I had to push everyone away, including the only woman to ever capture my attention.

Her comforting touches, kind words, and vibrant blue eyes were too much. Not enough. Confusing thoughts and feelings flashed back and forth in my mind, needing more, yet knowing I couldn't have it.

For one exhilarating, terrifying moment, Josephine saw everything. All of me. Whatever's left, anyway. Her gentle gaze held mine as her small hand curled around my fingers, and that was it. I gave my fucking heart and soul to her.

Instead of waiting for her to crush it, I sent her away.

Like I said. Moron over here.

What the hell do I do now?

The pitter-patter of little feet pulls me from my downward spiral. I was supposed to go up and talk to Kayla, but I've been wallowing instead. It felt appropriate, considering how much of a failure I've been today. I'm just so damn tired.

"Uncle Reed?" Kayla's voice sounds from the other side of the dining room. "Are you okay?"

I can't see her from where I'm sprawled out on the floor, but I pat the spot next to me, hoping she'll join me. "I'm okay, Kayla. Just feeling sorry for myself," I tell her truthfully.

My niece pads over to me, pausing briefly before flopping down with a sigh. *Same, kid. Same.*

"I'm sorry I snapped at you," I say, glancing over at her.

Kayla nods her head. "I'm sorry I said I hate you."

We lay there in silence for a few moments, then Kayla speaks up again.

"Is that it? Jo Jo said we had to say sorry and things would be better. Are they better?"

I chuckle at her innocent, heartfelt question. "I think so. I'm not very good at this stuff."

"Yeah. I know," she sighs.

I laugh again, then turn on my side, propping myself up on one elbow. Kayla smirks at me, and I return it. As per usual, Josephine was right. Kids talk a bunch of shit, but they don't seem to hold grudges for very long. Thank god.

"What did you paint today?" I ask, hoping to bridge the gap between us.

"The carpet," my niece deadpans.

My eyes widen, and then she bursts out laughing. She's sassy and sweet. I can see why she and Josephine connected right away.

I reach out and tickle Kayla, who thrashes around on the floor and tries to tickle me back. The little girl springs up and then pounces on me with a roar. I pretend to struggle for a few seconds, then scoop Kayla up and swing her in the air like I used to when she was smaller.

Kayla giggles, her green eyes filled with the kind of joy only kids seem to have. For once, I'm the one who put that look in her eyes. And I have Josephine to thank for that. Speaking of...

"Have you seen Jo Jo?" I ask Kayla once I set her down on the floor.

"She didn't come back?"

I furrow my brow. I didn't know she left in the first place. "Where did she go?"

Kayla looks down at her feet, shifting her weight from one foot to the other. "Um... I sort of lost my locket," she whispers, her hand instinctively going to her neck where she always has the golden heart-shaped locket. "We went on a walk this morning, way out to the big trees. I think it fell off there."

"The big trees... on the southside of the property?"

My niece shrugs because of course she has no idea in which direction the trees are located. Shit. That's at the edge of the property line. Any further, and they might have fallen in the little creek that always floods this time of year.

As if on cue, lightning flashes, making the room glow in an eerie electric purple. The thunderclap that follows rattles the windows, making Kayla squeak and jump.

"Jo Jo! She's out there! She's still out there!"

"Fuck," I mutter, running a hand through my hair.

Kayla starts crying, and I want to punch myself in the face. I need to be softer around her. Or, at the very least, stop cursing so much.

"Hey, honey, it's okay," I say, kneeling in front of her like I've seen Josephine do a thousand times. "We're safe here."

"I... I... kn-know..." she wails. "But what about Jo Jo?"

This girl. Such a big heart.

"I'm going to go look for her. You stay here and be a brave girl for me, okay? Let's get you set up in the basement." Kayla agrees and winds her little hand in mine, leading me downstairs.

Once she's settled under a blanket with the TV on, I run upstairs and grab a jacket, shoving my feet into an old pair of boots before racing out the door. I don't like leaving her alone, but I can't very well drag her outside into the storm. I know she's safe here in the basement, with the TV drowning out the sound of the thunder and lashing rain.

A wall of rain hits me as soon as I step outside, and I'm completely drenched. It only makes me more determined to find Josephine. What the hell was she thinking going out in this weather? Why didn't she ask for help?

Because you're an asshole who can't figure out how to tell a girl you like her.

Dammit.

I make my way past the swingset, my big feet caked with mud, but I keep going. Nothing can weigh me down. Nothing will stop me until I have Josephine in my arms.

Another flash of lightning streaks across the sky, followed by thunder cracking in the distance.

"Josephine!" I yell, though the rain drowns out most of the sound. "Hang on, sweetness," I call out, even if she can't hear me. I need her to know help is on the way. She might not want to see me after I made a fool of myself, but I need to get her to safety.

I swallow down the lump in my throat at the thought of any harm coming to her. Christ, if she fell, hit her head...

I growl, clenching my fists and pumping my arms as I sprint across the yard toward the back of the property. That can't happen. I won't accept it.

The sky lights up again, and this time, I can see the silhouette of someone limping toward me.

"Josephine!" I shout, seconds before thunder rumbles and shakes the earth.

I watch in horror as she stumbles forward, crashing on the ground with a thud.

I'm by her side in seconds, taking my jacket off and wrapping it around her before lifting her curvy body and crushing her against my chest.

"I f-found it," Josephine stutters out, her face ghostly pale except for her little nose, which is red with cold, and her eyes, rimmed in red as well.

"It doesn't matter," I grunt. She winces, and I want to bite my damn tongue off since it can't seem to communicate anything anyway. "You," grit out. "You matter. Only you, sweetness."

Her eyes go wide, her cute brow scrunching up in confusion. I bundle her up closer to me and start the walk back to the house in concentrated steps, not wanting to slip and damage my precious cargo.

Josephine buries her face into the side of my neck, and I tilt my head slightly, resting it on hers and blocking the rain as much as possible. She's shivering, and I can feel her heart beating out of control. My woman is freezing, scraped up, bruised, and hurt. Because of me. Because I snapped, and she didn't feel like she could ask for help.

We finally reach the house, and I carry her inside, straight upstairs to the en suite bathroom in my bedroom. I hear Kayla pitter-pattering behind us, and when I set Josephine down on the sink counter, my niece wedges herself between her nanny and me.

"Jo Jo, are you hurt? I'm sorry. I'm so sorry I made you go," she cries as she wraps her arms around Josephine's waist.

"I-I'm f-fine," Josephine says, her teeth chattering with each word.

I rub Kayla's back, then pry her off. "Why don't you go grab some warm pajamas from my top drawer for Jo Jo to change into?" Kayla nods, satisfied to have a mission. Girl after my own heart.

When she finally walks off, I step closer, cupping Josephine's face in my hands.

"I'm so sorry, baby," I say brokenly. "What hurts? What can I do? God, Jo…"

My woman covers my hands with her own, her shallow breathing slowly returning to normal. I keep my eyes trained on her, ready to do her bidding as soon as she tells me how I can help. I need a job. I need to start to make this up to her.

"I'm ok-kay," she whispers, blinking her big blue eyes open. "I tripped over a tree r-root on my way back to the house. My ankle hurts, but it-t's not a big deal."

I press a kiss to her forehead, then release my hold on her, kneeling to inspect her ankles. I hiss out a breath when I see her left ankle already a red, swollen mess.

"Josephine," I murmur, my eyes trailing up her legs, taking note of her scraped-up knees. Continuing my survey of damages, I see little scratches and bruises on her arms, each one like a knife in my gut.

Standing up, I reach behind me and grab a fluffy towel. Gently, so damn gently, I dry Josephine's hair, face, arms, and anywhere else she'll let me.

"Here," Kayla announces as she steps into the bathroom. She sets the clean clothes on the counter then stands next to me, inspecting Josephine's ankle.

I don't want her to feel even worse about this situation than she already does so I give her another mission. "Thank you, Kayla. Can you go get some comfy blankets and pillows out on the couch for Jo Jo? Then go on and get ready for bed. I'll heat up a late dinner for you while Josephine gets cleaned up, okay?"

Kayla nods then gives Josephine the saddest smile in the world.

"I'm okay," Josephine promises. "And look, I have your locket."

Kayla sniffles and holds out her hand, taking the locket from Jo. "Thank you."

Josephine smiles, and I shoo Kayla out before returning my focus to my woman.

Kneeling once more, I lift her sore foot in my hand, carefully removing her shoe and sock. It doesn't look broken, though she'll likely have a bruise there for a few weeks. I take off her other shoe and sock, then clean the cuts on her knees. They aren't too deep, thank god, but it pains me to see them all the same.

"Can you stand, baby?" I ask, peering into her eyes for the first time since focusing on her wounds.

She's staring at me with an unreadable expression. Is she mad at me? She has every right to be.

Finally, Josephine nods her head once. "Yeah. I..." She blows out a shuddering breath. "I don't think anyone's ever... never mind."

She doesn't have to finish her sentence for me to know what she was thinking. No one has ever taken care of her like this. It's a first for me as well, but I vow to do better at showing her how much she means to me. I've done a shit job so far, but that all changes today. Right now.

I ease her off the counter, gently setting her down on the floor. She wobbles slightly, and I pull her against me, holding her trembling body close. "I've got you, sweetness," I whisper.

I wish we could stay wrapped up in each other's embrace for hours, but Josephine is still cold and wet and in need of a hot shower. Reluctantly, I pull away from my woman, leaning to the side and turning on the water for the shower.

"Get warmed up, then come meet me in the living room. I'll wrap your ankle, and we'll talk."

I hoped my words would be comforting, but instead, Josephine dips her head down, her hair covering her face. "Okay," she whispers.

"Jo..." God, I wish I could strip her down and step in the shower with her. Not in a sexual way, not yet, at least. I just want to hold her, feel her, and take care of her every need.

I grip her chin between my thumb and forefinger, the same way I did that first morning after the French toast disaster. Tipping her head up, I'm hit with clear blue eyes, brimming with tears. "Baby, you're killing me. Wash up, and come find me. We'll talk," I say again, hoping it puts her at ease. We'll talk about what an idiot I am and what I can do to make sure she stays here with Kayla and me. Forever.

Josephine nods then wraps her arms around herself. I hate that she looks like she's protecting herself from me, but it's nothing less than I deserve.

Every step away from her is excruciating, but we both need to change clothes and get warmed up before I spill my heart out to her. Plus, I need to get Kayla off to bed with some food in her stomach. I know she'll want to talk to Josephine, but I'll convince her to wait until morning.

Everyone needs a good night's sleep. I'm hoping I can convince my Josephine to spend it in my arms.

Chapter 7

We'll talk.

A shiver runs down my spine, but not from the cold. I'm surrounded by steam and hot water, but Reed's words cut through me like icicles. He's going to let me go. I know it.

And why wouldn't he? I set his kitchen on fire, I destroyed his carpet, and then I went and got stranded on the far side of the property, making Reed come collect me and pick up my mess, yet again.

I rinse the conditioner out of my hair, closing my eyes and letting the water pour over me.

God, the way Reed scooped me up in his arms as if I weighed nothing, how safe I felt when he clutched me to his chest... I'll never forget a single moment with him, even if he kicks me out tonight.

He looked so worried. No, not worried. *Wrecked.* For a moment, I fantasized about him being upset because I was hurt. When he knelt in front of me and tended to my wounds, I thought I saw guilt tugging at his features, but that doesn't make sense.

And when he pressed his lips to my forehead... I must have imagined that.

I stand under the water for a few more minutes until my fingers are pruney and the air is thick with steam. I can't avoid *the talk* any longer. Surely, he won't kick me out tonight. Not during a storm like this. But tomorrow...

Shutting off the water, I carefully step out of the shower, grabbing a huge fuzzy towel hanging on the wall. I wince as I put weight on my left ankle, but it's already feeling better after the shower.

I stare at the nicely folded pajama pants and sweatshirt Kayla grabbed for me. Reed said to get them from his room. I wonder why.

Lifting the sweatshirt, I hold it up to my body, noting that it will go down to my knees. The pajama pants are big as well, and I have to roll the waistband a few times to get them to stay up.

I love the way his clothes smell, masculine and earthy. I love the way they feel, rubbing against my skin. It's silly, but I like knowing Reed wore this. I might have to steal it after he fires me. A little token to remember him by.

And just like that, all my nice thoughts are gone. Time to face the music.

Opening the door, I take one step into the hallway before Reed pops up from his spot on the floor, right next to the bathroom door. What is he doing? How long has he been sitting there?

"Josephine," he rumbles. "Thought you could use some help on the stairs."

I don't have time to respond before I'm being lifted into Reed's arms once more. I automatically curl up against him, savoring his touch. Reed lets out a satisfied-sounding grunt, almost like he's doing the same.

"I can walk down the stairs," I inform him, even as I rest my head on his shoulder.

He doesn't say anything as he carries me through the house, finally settling me on a chair in the dining room. There's a cup of hot chocolate and a bowl of soup waiting for me. That has to be a good sign, right?

"Eat," Reed says, towering over me.

"Are you going to just stand there and watch me?" I probably shouldn't be poking the bear, but I can't help it with Reed. I like pushing his buttons.

He grunts then storms out. Shit.

A moment later, the growly man returns with a fleece blanket from the couch. He drapes it around my shoulders then nods to himself before taking the seat next to me.

"Thanks," I whisper.

I take a few sips of hot chocolate, then get to work on the soup. I need something to do while Reed is just sitting here, staring.

"More?" he asks when I've finished the first bowl in a matter of minutes.

I shake my head no, then finish off the hot chocolate. If I have any more to eat, I might get sick to my stomach when he fires me.

Reed surprises me by resting his large, warm hand over mine, curling his fingers into my palm and squeezing.

"I'm so sorry, sweetness," he whispers.

I blink a few times, not sure I heard him right. "Sorry?"

Reed winces. "Yeah. I'm sorry for everything. I'm sorry I snapped earlier. I'm sorry I'm an asshole and made you think you couldn't ask for my help with the necklace."

Whoa. What's happening? He's... apologizing?

"Reed, it's not your fault–"

"I'm so fucking sorry you got hurt, baby. I'm sorry I'm a confusing jerk who can't seem to get anything right. I..." he sighs heavily, running a hand through his already wild hair.

I'm confused, but more than that, I want to comfort this man. He's absolutely ruined, sitting here, tripping over his words, shame and remorse dripping from each one.

My hand finds his, our fingers twining together. Reed stares at our connected hands then slowly drags his eyes up to meet mine. The pain in his gaze makes my chest ache. I have to swallow down a lump in my throat to keep from crying.

When he speaks again, his tone is hushed like he's not sure he's ready to confess his thoughts.

"I don't know what I'm doing, Josephine," he murmurs. "I don't know how to be a parent. I don't know how to be a partner. I don't know how to tell you how incredible you are, how precious and important you've become to me."

"Reed," I whisper through tears. Is this really happening?

"Let me finish, sweetness," he says with a nervous smile. His cheeks are flushed and his green eyes are filled with vulnerability. "You... fuck, I'm not good at expressing myself, but you make me want to be better. I want to be able to share myself with you, and with Kayla. You're so good with her, so open and caring. You've taught me that showing emotion isn't a weakness. Sometimes it's our greatest strength. I just... I don't know how. Show me, Josephine. Show me how to love you."

Love?

I stand from my chair and close the distance between us, stepping between Reed's parted thighs. He peers up at me in surprise, then a look of awe crosses his face like he can't believe I want to be closer to him.

I cup his cheeks like he's done to me before. Reed closes his eyes and breathes in deeply as if capturing my scent and recording it to memory. When he blinks his eyes open, there's a determined, possessive edge to his green depths.

He curls his fingers around the back of my neck and draws me closer so our foreheads are touching.

"You already know how to love," I whisper, my lips barely brushing his. "Just give yourself permission to trust. Do you trust me?"

"Yes," comes his automatic response.

I can't contain my smile, but before I can say anything else, he fuses his mouth to mine. Reed parts my lips and licks inside my mouth, tangling our tongues together. I moan at the desperate, empty throbbing in my core, needing so much more from him.

Reed swallows down my desperate cry, muffling the sound and pulling my body closer against his. I can feel the tight muscles he has packed into his chest and stomach.

He deepens the kiss, pulling me onto his lap so I'm straddling him. I feel his hands everywhere, sliding under the shirt I'm wearing, caressing my back, hips, and thighs. His large fingers roam over my skin in the lightest of touches and then dig into my flesh, rocking me against his hardening cock.

"Fuck," he grunts into my neck before kissing me there. "You're so fucking soft," he groans, trailing more kisses down my neck and shoulder.

Reed stands up abruptly, keeping me in his arms as he turns and sets me down on the table. I squeal at the sudden movement, but he captures the sound in his mouth, sucking all the air out of my lungs in a punishing, devastating kiss.

He grips my inner thighs and spreads my legs apart so he can get closer to my aching core. Reed grinds his thick dick against me and tangles his fingers in my hair, ripping my mouth away from his and nipping at my jaw.

A shiver runs through me when he covers the little bite with a sweet kiss. He's dominant, demanding, and territorial while also being tender and caring. It's addictive, the way he handles me.

"Need to taste more of you," Reed groans.

I'm so lost in the way his cock is rubbing against my throbbing clit, I hardly register his words. I nod my head, knowing I'll like whatever Reed does next.

To my complete shock, he grips the neckline of the shirt I'm wearing and tears it in two. I gasp and giggle at his eagerness but then moan when I feel his tongue circling my nipple. Reed grunts and licks the other one before closing his lips around it and sucking. Hard.

I squeeze my thighs around his hips and lean back on my hands, giving him more access. His hands and mouth cover every inch of my breasts and torso with kisses, bites, pinches, and soothing strokes.

Reed scrapes his teeth down my soft belly and kneels in front of me, shouldering my knees apart so he's staring right at my pussy. I know he sees how shamefully wet I am. I've soaked through the thin pajama pants he gave me.

Reed leans forward and covers the wet spot with his mouth, sucking on the fabric and making me gasp in surprise. He grunts into my pussy and breathes in deep. Holy hell, this man is fucking hot. Everything he does.

Reed hooks his thumbs into the side of my pants and slowly drags them down my legs until I'm bare before him. For a few seconds, he just stares at me. It's unnerving. No one has ever seen me like this. Touched me like this. Ruined me like this.

He peppers kisses up the insides of my thighs, first one and then the other. Then he parts my lips with his thumbs and lets out a strangled moan.

"Jesus Christ, you're dripping for me. I need it. Need to taste it. Need to." He sounds like a man possessed. I love it. How am I the one doing this to him? Why me?

I don't have time to overthink it before his tongue slides through my folds. I gasp and moan, falling backward onto the table. Reed licks me up and down, humming into my pussy like it's the best thing he's ever tasted. I swear I feel his wet, hot tongue deep in my core, the liquid heat pooling inside me and filling my veins with burning ecstasy.

Reed leans back slightly, and I whimper at the loss of him. Then he swipes two fingers up my slit, pulling my pussy lips open and forming a cage around my clit with his fingers. My eyes slam shut as his tongue makes contact with my isolated bundle of nerves.

The whole world zooms down to just Reed and me. He sucks down on me fiercely, and I feel my body wind up fast and hard. When I'm about to come, he backs away and pushes his tongue inside me, lapping at my throbbing channel. One finger finds my clit and he brushes it softly, never letting me go over the edge but making sure I'm still right there.

"Please, please..." I whine, squirming beneath him and trying to get him where I need him most.

Reed ignores me, continuing to torture my swollen, sensitive cunt with his tongue. I feel his finger circling my entrance, over and over, then dipping inside. I moan, feeling my tight channel stretch around his large digit. Fuck, I can't even imagine what his cock is going to feel like. I don't know if I'll survive, but I sure as hell want to try.

He slowly works his finger in and out of me with gentle thrusts, then he curls it up. Holy. Fucking. Shit. My body spasms violently, causing my thighs to close around his head and my back to bow off the table.

"Feel good?" he asks, his voice low and gravelly, sending another shiver up my spine.

"So...good..." I gasp.

Reed grunts and then curls his finger up again and rubs that spot, then taps it over and over.

"Reed! Reed...I..."

He fingerfucks me hard and sucks on my clit, growling into my pussy. My muscles lock up tight, each thrust and rough lick sending me higher, higher, higher...

And then I shatter.

I scream out his name and claw at the table as my orgasm ravishes me. Reed slides his hands underneath my ass and pulls me closer, burying his face into my pulsing cunt and drinking down all of my release. I squeeze my eyes shut and fall into pleasure so intense I think I might pass out.

"You're okay, baby. I've got you."

I open my eyes, noticing I'm on the couch, covered in a blanket and curled up in Reed's lap. "I... What?"

He chuckles softly, the hearty sound traveling through my body, warming up my bones. "You passed out on me for a second. Are you okay? Was that too much?" His amused look turns serious. "Did I hurt you? How's your ankle? Did you–"

I cut him off with a kiss, threading my fingers in his hair and letting him know that I'm perfectly fine with every stroke of my tongue.

"I'm good," I breathe out once we break apart.

Reed lets out a satisfied huff, then stands, cradling me against his expansive chest, packed with muscle. I love it. I love that he wants to carry me everywhere. As a bigger girl, I never thought I'd have that. I never thought I'd want it, either, but with Reed... I love the way he handles me.

"Where are we going?" I ask when we're halfway up the stairs.

"Bed. I need to hold you."

I squirm in his embrace, and Reed stops, looking down at me.

"Just cuddling tonight, sweetness," he says sternly, reading my lustful thoughts. "You need rest."

I pout, but Reed just kisses the tip of my nose and continues to his bedroom. He sets me down gently, unwrapping me from one blanket just so he can tuck me in and wrap another blanket around me. He's so gentle in the way he's caring for me. I've never experienced anything like it.

Once I'm all snuggled up, Reed looks at me, then at his dresser. I know what he's debating, but I can make the decision easy for him.

"I want to feel you," I whisper, my cheeks burning at my confession. "When you're holding me," I clarify. "Um, so, you don't have to... wear anything. If you don't want to," I add quickly.

The grin that spreads across his face is enough to make me wet all over again. Good lord, this man. Everything he does is addicting.

"You don't have to ask me twice, baby. Scoot over."

I make room for Reed while watching him strip down. *Yum.* Muscles stacked on muscles, abs for days, and yes, yes, yes... he drops his boxers, letting me see all of him.

My jaw drops, making Reed chuckle. Holy crap. I know we're not doing anything tonight, but whenever it's time to fit that monster inside me... I can't wait.

"Be a good girl and roll over on your other side," Reed says. "If you keep looking at me like that, I might have to do something about this," he rasps, fisting his cock and giving it one long stroke.

I start to nod my head, but Reed shakes his no, then motions for me to roll on my side again. I reluctantly tear my eyes away from his flawless body, then smile when I feel the bed dip down with his weight.

Reed pulls me into his arms, my back pressed against his front. Every place of contact sizzles, sending awareness to every muscle, every nerve, every cell.

"Get some rest, baby," he whispers into the shell of my ear. "I'll be right here."

I hum contentedly, and snuggle deeper. Reed wraps an arm around my waist, keeping me anchored to him while he brushes a kiss to my temple and the back of my neck. My eyes flutter closed and I relax into his embrace, feeling more at peace than I ever have.

Chapter 8

"Here's my cell number and my home phone," I tell Mrs. Brady as I hand her a piece of paper.

"We'll be fine, but I'll keep these on the fridge just in case," she says before smiling down at Kayla. "Maddy is so excited you could come to her slumber party! The other girls are downstairs playing dress-up if you want to join."

Kayla spins around and gives me a big hug before skipping down the hall. "Have fun!" I call after her. Turning back to Mrs. Brady, I give her a nod. "It's her first sleepover," I confide.

"It is for a lot of the girls. They'll be fine, but I know where to reach you if Kayla ends up wanting to go home early."

Kayla's bubbly laughter echoes up the stairs, and then she chatters away with the other girls about costumes and doing makeovers later.

"I don't think we'll have a problem there," I say with a smile. We shake hands and I let myself out, trying not to run to my car. Tonight, I have Josephine all to myself.

I'm so proud of Kayla for wanting to go to this party and hang out with her friends. Switching schools was a difficult transition, and I worried she wouldn't like her teachers or make any friends. However, since Josephine came into our lives, Kayla has let down her defenses. She's made several friends, including Maddy, who insisted she come for a slumber party.

I zip through a yellow light and pick up speed, needing to be home with my woman. It's been a week since I've had her naked and stretched out, which is too damn long, in my opinion. We've shared a few kisses before bed, but Josephine was still healing from her injuries, and I already felt like a beast for devouring her sweet little pussy on the kitchen table. The next time I have her wet and aching, it will be on my bed, where she'll be more comfortable.

Pulling into my driveway, I throw the car in park and leap out. I don't care how desperate I look. I just want to be with my Josephine.

When I step inside, the smell of savory Italian food hits me, and I follow it into the kitchen. Josephine is setting the table, and I walk up to her, circling my arms around her waist and pulling her into me.

"Reed–"

I take her lips for my own, drinking down her words. She gasps softly, then wiggles against me, rubbing herself up and down my hardening cock. I dig my fingers into her hips, helping her grind down as I ravish her mouth.

Josephine tips her head up, breaking our kiss to gulp down air. I trail my lips down her throat, nipping her sensitive flesh and licking away the sting.

"Dinner smells good," I murmur into her skin.

Josephine laughs softly, and I smile into the side of her neck.

"Shocking, right?" she teases. "I had it delivered, so don't be too impressed."

"Mmm, sweetness, you always impress me," I grumble before taking her lips again.

Josephine wraps her arms around my shoulders, and I trail my hands down her back, gripping her ass and lifting her, crushing her soft curves into the hard planes of my body.

"Screw dinner," Josephine says into the shell of my ear, her tone desperate and demanding.

"I'd rather screw you," I respond, making her smirk.

I pull away from my woman, though she's still in my arms. I regain enough of my senses to start navigating my way upstairs. I stumble through the kitchen, only making it up three steps before I have to stop and press Josephine against the wall, covering her mouth with mine. She rolls her hips, making me growl as her hot, wet core scrapes against my jean-covered cock.

"Need you," I growl, sucking on her collarbone and licking a stripe up her throat.

"Y-yes," she pants, her thighs flexing around my hips. "Please, Reed. Please make me yours."

"Fuck yes," I groan, peeling her off the wall so I can continue our journey upstairs to bed. I'd love to take her up against the wall one day, but my woman deserves better for our first time.

I somehow make it to the bedroom without tearing both of our clothes off. Setting Josephine down next to the bed, I take my time peppering her with kisses and tracing my fingers over her exposed skin. She shivers and exhales forcefully before gasping for air. So damn responsive.

"I, um…" she pants, taking a step back. Josephine rests a hand on my chest, staring at it instead of looking me in the eye.

"What is it, love? Is this too fast? Too much? I want you, sweetness, but I can wait until–"

"No!" she exclaims passionately, her eyes meeting mine and making me grin. "No, I don't want to stop. God, please don't stop." She's still a little breathless, her cheeks flushed and lips swollen. So beautiful. "I just… you should probably know something."

"Whatever it is, you can tell me," I say softly.

Josephine takes a deep breath, then blurts out, "I'm a virgin." Her eyes squeeze shut, and every muscle in her body tenses.

"Fuck, yes," I grunt, nuzzling into her neck and pulling her flush against my body. "Mine," I say into her soft skin. "All mine, sweetness. I haven't been with anyone in years. Over a decade. Can't remember anything or anyone before you."

"You're not… disappointed?" she asks tentatively.

"Disappointed?" I lean back, getting a good look at those big blue eyes. "Never," I growl. "I love that I'll be your first. Your goddamn only, too."

Josephine nods, the tension finally draining from her features, replaced by a wicked smile. I'm so gone for this girl. Head over fuckin' heels.

Slowly, I strip every piece of clothing from her luscious body, pausing to nip and kiss her plump flesh. So soft and sweet.

"*Mine*," I say as I help her lay down on the bed with her legs dangling over the edge.

I kneel in front of my beautiful girl, lifting one leg over my shoulder and then the other. Gripping her hips to keep her in place, I run my nose along the seam of her pussy. I blow hot air over her juicy folds and feel her tremble in my hands. My tongue dips into her soaking wet entrance and up, up, up to her tight ball of nerves.

"Oh, fuck, Reed…" she cries out, clenching her thighs together when I circle her clit. Another forceful stroke of my tongue pushes through her folds, pulling whimpers from deep within her.

I spear my tongue into her hole, sipping her sweet nectar straight from the source. Massaging the walls of her velvet pussy, I get lost in her scent, her taste, her essence as it gushes over my lips, dripping down my chin. I find her clit and circle around the outside, not quite giving her what she needs.

"Ohmygod, Reed, *please*…" Josephine rotates her hips, trying to get me to touch her where she needs me. I place my other hand over her stomach, spreading out my fingers and pinning her in place.

I withdraw my hand completely and look up at her, depriving her of my touch altogether. She whimpers in frustration.

"Tsk, tsk, Josephine. You take what I give you, do you understand?" She nods. "Good girl. I'll always give you what you need."

Diving back into her addictive pussy, I swirl my tongue around her little button, tracing patterns and switching between feather-soft licks and hard, forceful licks. Josephine writhes beautifully under me as I continue my assault.

I move my fingers to her entrance, slipping one finger into her tight channel.

"*Reed,*" she shouts as she fists the sheets in her hands.

I pump my digit in and out of her, curling my finger to massage her most sensitive spot. I thrust two fingers inside her and watch as she shakes and jerks her hips up at the invasion. Leaning back, I watch my fingers move in and out of her as she rides my hand. Fucking beautiful.

She's so close. I feel her muscles tense, her pussy pulsing around me. Her body is strung tight, vibrating with tension as I wind her up with each pump of my fingers.

"Ohmygod, ohmygod, Reed, I... Ohmygod..."

She can barely form words as she reaches her peak, her breathing becoming more and more erratic.

"I've got you, love. Come for me. I need you to come."

I lean back down and suck her clit into my mouth, massaging it with my tongue. I bite down on her hard nub and she explodes on my hand, gushing and thrashing and crying out my name. I replace my fingers with my tongue and lap up wave after wave of wetness as her pussy convulses and she rides out her high.

I rub her clit again and again in continuous, steady circles, then pump two fingers inside her swollen, throbbing pussy. I'm mesmerized by her soft, pink folds, glistening with her need. She's so fucking wet, my fingers glide easily in and out of her, stretching her and preparing her for my huge cock.

Soon, Josephine tenses up against my hand and I know she's on edge.

"That's it, baby. Let go for me. I've got you."

I curl my fingers up to hit her G-spot and press down on her clit with my thumb and she spasms around my hand, every muscle in her body clenching before her great release.

"Oh, fuck! Reed, Reed, Reed..." she chants as she floats back down to earth. I stare at her, soaking in every facial expression, every curve of her body, every bounce of her gorgeous tits as she trembles before me.

I remove my fingers from her and circle her nipples, covering her in her sweet honey before licking it off her breasts. I work my way up her chest, nipping and kissing the graceful curve of her neck, relishing in the slightly salty taste of her skin from the thin sheen of sweat covering her body. I love that I put it there. Made her sweat, moan, and shake.

Finally, my lips graze the delicate shell of her ear. "Fucking beautiful, Josephine. So perfect."

I hold Josephine in my arms until her breathing finally returns to normal. Her brilliant eyes flutter open, making me groan when I see the lust still burning there.

Good.

I'm not done with her. Not by a long shot.

"No fair," she pouts, sitting up to tug on my shirt. "You've seen all of me, but I've hardly seen any of you."

I grin at her, loving her eagerness. "As you wish, my love. Anything you want."

I crawl off the bed and pull my shirt over my head. Josephine props herself up on her elbows to watch me. I've never been insecure about my looks. I don't consider myself a vain person, but when Josephine looks at me, I wonder what she thinks.

I start on the button of my jeans as she sits up on the bed. My pants drop to the ground and I hook my thumbs in my boxers. Josephine gets up on her knees and walks to the edge of the bed to where I'm standing. Before I can take my underwear off, she places her hands on my chest.

I stare down at her, my skin burning under her touch. Her eyes glide over my chest, arms, and stomach. She traces the swirls of ink on my skin, leaving behind a trail of fire as she goes. Josephine traces her lips over my heart, placing a sweet kiss there. I know she can feel it pounding in my chest, every beat pulsing with need, desire, and love.

"Mine," she whispers into my skin before resting her forehead there.

I am overwhelmed by her love, her sweet, tender touches, her soft exploration. I place two fingers under her chin and tilt her head up towards mine before brushing my lips on hers. She opens immediately for me and I dive into her soft mouth. Her hands move up my chest and around my neck, tangling in the hair at the back of my head as she tugs me closer, trying to devour me.

Suddenly she pulls away from me and I follow her like a magnet, drawn to her light, her touch. Her hands glide back down my body and she pulls at my underwear. I let her undress me and carefully watch her face as my cock springs into view.

"Holy shit," she whispers in awe.

"Agreed," I tell her with a sly smirk. "You're so fucking beautiful, sweetheart. So perfect. So mine." My eyes sweep over her body, and I can't believe all of this is for me.

I dip my head down and kiss her, sucking her tongue into my mouth and stroking it with mine. We break for air and I lick down her throat, feeling her pulse race under my tongue. I reach down and drag a finger through her slit, collecting her juices and checking her readiness.

"So wet for me, love."

She nods, her eyes glazed over with lust. I trace my fingers over her lips, rubbing her honey across her soft skin before licking and kissing it off. She moans, and the sound goes straight to my dick. My dirty girl likes it.

I reach down again and gather more of her sweet cum, rubbing it on my aching cock in long strokes. I line myself up to her entrance and gaze into her captivating green eyes, searching for any doubts or worries.

"Are you ready for me, love?"

She nods.

"I need your words. I need to hear you say it."

"I want you, Reed. Please, I'm ready for you. I want to be yours completely."

Her confession does me in. I growl and push the head of my cock into her tight, hot pussy. "I'll be gentle, love. I promise. You're safe with me," I comfort her. I know it's going to hurt, and I hate that thought. But I love knowing I'll be the one to make it better.

"I know. I'm ready. Please, please, Reed. I ache for you."

Fuck. That's all I need to hear. I push myself further into her, bottoming out in one long thrust. She whimpers and clings to me, squeezing her eyes shut as a single tear escapes. My heart clenches knowing I caused her pain. I kiss her tear away and nuzzle her neck.

"Thank you, love. Thank you for giving me this precious gift," I whisper into her soft, warm skin. "Are you okay?" I lean back and search her face.

"I'm so full. I love being connected to you like this." I feel her squeeze her pussy around my girth and I almost come right then.

"Fuck, baby girl, you feel so incredible. Love having you wrapped around me, love filling you up." My cock twitches, pre-cum no doubt leaking out into her pussy. "I have to move. Are you okay?" I ask again. I might die if I don't start moving, but I'd happily die right here if she wasn't ready.

She moves her hips in answer to my question, wriggling beneath me.

I growl and pull out of her slowly. Looking down, I see the evidence of her virginity smeared on my cock, blood mixing with her cum. I grow impossibly harder as I ease back into her.

Setting a steady pace, I pump in and out of her, watching her perfect pussy stretch and swallow me each time. It's so fucking hot, I never want to look away. At the same time, I need to see Josephine's face, need to gaze at her gorgeous body, need to see and suck and feel every inch of her. I want all of her, and I want it right fucking now.

I pull my eyes away from where we are joined and look into her eyes. I see the same need in her, the need to possess every inch, to wring out every ounce of pleasure from our bodies.

She leans up and kisses me, biting my lip and dragging it through her teeth. I growl and thrust into her harder. She moans and drags her fingernails down my back.

"Fuck, baby girl, yes. Mark me, make me yours."

"Ye-yes, yes, oh fuck..." She moans as I angle my hips to hit her sweet spot. "More...I need..."

She doesn't even finish her thought before I lean back on my heels and throw one of her legs over my shoulder and then the other. The new angle takes me deeper, makes her tighter, squeezing my dick in a sweet torture. I thrust into her again and again, folding her in half.

"Jesus, fuck, Josephine. Fuck, you feel so good, baby."

"Reed! Oh yessss..." Her head thrashes back and forth as her mouth drops open in a silent scream.

I plunge into her again and again. She's like nothing I've ever experienced before. It's overwhelming. Her eagerness to open up to me, to take whatever I give her, to trust me completely with her body. It's fucking everything.

I feel so goddamn good as the tingle in my spine starts, hurtling me towards an orgasm. I'm almost afraid of when it hits. I can already tell it's going to be bigger and better than anything I've ever experienced.

"Reed, I....Oh, god," she gasps for air, "I'm..."

She's shaking and pulsing, her muscles taut and strained.

"That's it, love, I've got you."

I pick up my pace, chasing our release, needing it while at the same time never wanting this to end. I reach down and rub her clit furiously, needing her to come before I do.

"Ah, ah, ah, fuck, fuck!" Josephine pants as she meets me thrust for thrust.

"Come for me. Come all over my big fat cock, Josephine. Let me feel that pussy pop."

I pinch her clit and feel her walls snap around my dick, squeezing me painfully in the best possible way. Josephine screams and gushes all over me. I drop her legs back down to either side of my hips and lean over her again, swallowing her moans and cries of ecstasy.

I pound into her, our juices flowing and making obscene sounds as our bodies collide again and again. I still inside of her as my cock swells. Roaring my release, wave after wave of cum pours out of me. I continue to thrust as I empty myself inside her. Josephine comes again, one orgasm rolling into another as we throb and pulse together, our bodies dripping in sweat.

I collapse, rolling onto my side and pulling her with me. We're both gasping for air and shaking. She's incredible.

"Goddamn, Josephine. Just...goddamn." I lean down and kiss the top of her head. I panic when she doesn't say anything or look up at me. I panic. "Are you okay? I wasn't gentle. Fuck, I said I'd be careful. Please forgive me..."

Josephine tilts her head up and kisses me, cutting me off mid-sentence.

"I'm more than okay, Reed. I feel perfect. Complete. I have no words." She buries her head in my chest, relief washing over me. "Thank you," she whispers.

I wrap my arms around her and hold her tight. This feels like home. I stroke her back, tracing circles and patterns into her soft skin. She rests her cheek on my chest and I feel her breath tickle across my skin.

Josephine is asleep within seconds and I have to chuckle. I love knowing I fucked her so good she was drained of all of her energy. My girl has quite the stamina, but I like knowing I wore her out.

Chapter 9

I slowly blink my eyes open, wincing at my sore muscles as I stretch. Why do I feel like I ran a marathon yesterday?

And then I remember. *Reed.*

More awareness floods into my brain and I realize I'm curled up next to him, my arm flung over his torso, and my head resting against his shoulder.

The hand I have on his chest slowly slides down his freaking gorgeous body. I mean, seriously, the man is all muscle and sex appeal. I still can't believe he wants *me*, that he finds *me* beautiful.

I slip my hand further down, wrapping my fingers around his thick cock. I love that he's already hard for me like he's been dreaming about me as much as I've dreamed about him these last few weeks.

His muscles tense and I hear a soft groan fall from his lips. I look up to find Reed still asleep. I shuffle down his body and get on my knees so I'm bent over him. Then, I lick his shaft from top to bottom, loving how his hips automatically thrust up to get closer to my mouth.

"Mmm... Josephine..." he mumbles in his sleep.

Encouraged by his groans, though spoken unconsciously, I open my mouth and suck just the head of his length inside. I look up at Reed right as his eyes snap open.

"Jesus Christ, Josephine." I pop off of his dick, wondering if I did something wrong. "Don't you dare stop now, sweetheart. Need those lips around my cock."

I smile and crawl in between his legs to give me better access. I stick out my tongue and lick him again, like a lollipop, flicking my tongue across the head again and again before dipping it inside the slit on top.

Reed roars, and I smirk. I love giving him pleasure like this, seeing him almost out of control. I open my mouth wide and descend on his thickness, taking him as far as I can. Massaging the vein running along the bottom of his shaft, I begin to suck and slowly pull back out. I bob my head up and down while Reed grunts and fists my hair, guiding my movements.

"That's it, baby. Just like that. You feel so good."

I hum around his dick and he growls, thrusting up and shoving his cock further in my mouth until it hits the back of my throat. I gag a little, and he combs his fingers through my hair.

"Relax, love. Breathe through your nose and open up that little throat of yours."

I do as he says and feel him going down my throat. I swallow on instinct and he growls again. When I get a good rhythm going, I reach down and take his balls in one hand, massaging them and sending a shiver through his entire body.

His hands tangle in my hair and try pulling me off. I grip his thighs and hold myself to him, taking him as deep as I can. His praise encourages me to keep going, suck harder, faster, give him as much pleasure as he's given me these last twelve hours.

"Shit! I'm coming, Josephine. I'm—"

Hot, salty liquid shoots down my throat, again and again. I swallow everything he gives me while he continues to grunt out his orgasm. When he's done, I pull back, releasing his cock with a pop. I lick him clean and then sit back on my heels to look at him.

His eyes are closed and he looks totally peaceful. I love knowing I did that to him, that I have the power to make him crazy with need, and then to relax him completely. Suddenly, his eyes snap open and I can tell he's hungry again.

"Come here, Josephine. Need your lips on mine right the fuck now."

I crawl up his body, kissing and licking every muscle I see along the way. Straddling him, I lean down and place my hands on either side of his head. Reed wastes no time. He cups the back of my neck and pulls me down, crashing his lips on mine. He owns this kiss, licking and sucking and driving me wild with need.

When we finally come up for air, I rest my forehead on his, both of us panting.

"Jesus, what a way to wake up." He looks at me with wonder and satisfaction.

"So it was okay? I mean, I've never done that before."

"Better than anything I could have ever dreamed."

I kiss him before he can see the tears welling up in my eyes at his compliment. The depth of feelings I already have for this man should scare me, but I don't have time to worry when Reed opens up and lets me lead us in a slow kiss. I want to believe everything he's told me in the last few days, but there's a little voice in the back of my head telling me this is only temporary.

Our kiss gives way to so much more as I start moving my hips. Reed's hands glide down my back, cupping my bare ass and pulling me closer, urging me to grind down on him with my soaking wet pussy.

He breaks the kiss only to attach his mouth to my neck, licking and nipping and kissing down to my shoulder.

"Are you still sore, baby?" he mumbles into my skin.

"No, I need you."

"Need you too, Josephine." He lifts me by my hips, hovering me over his already hard dick. "Ride my fucking cock like a good girl."

I moan at his words and sink down on his hard shaft.

Reed hisses out a breath once I'm fully seated on him. I wiggle my hips, getting used to feeling him like this. Then, I lift up on my knees until he's almost all the way out and impale myself on him.

"Josephine," He growls. "So good, baby."

I continue bouncing up and down, grinding my hips each time, hitting my clit on his pubic bone. Reed leans forward, sucking one of my breasts in his mouth while squeezing and kneading the other one.

"Ah, yes, yes…" I moan. He switches, licking and kissing his way over to my other breast.

"Fucking love these tits, baby." Reed pushes them together and licks up my cleavage.

I moan at his dirty words, more of my arousal leaking out of me. I love it. My eyes close and my hands find their way to my breasts as I knead them and pluck at my nipples. My nerves tingle, my muscles tense, my movements become jerky.

"That's it, baby. Take what you need from me."

I roll my hips two more times and then throw my head back, crying out as my orgasm slams into me. Reed grabs my hips and continues a relentless pace as he fucks up into me, riding out my orgasm.

I'm still coming down when I feel us shift, Reed flipping me on my back and pressing me into the bed. He's still deep inside me as he gathers my wrists in one of his large hands and pins them above my head.

"Gonna fuck you nice and hard, baby. After you come on my cock again, I'm gonna stick my dick in those luscious tits."

"Yes, please," I pant out. *Holy hell.* I didn't know I was into that, but I feel another wave of pleasure pushing to the surface, ready to break at the thought of him handling me like that.

Reed growls and leans down to kiss me. It's messy and passionate and perfect. Then, he leans back on his heels and guides one of my legs over his shoulder, and then the other. He pulls out and slams into me, letting out a primal noise as he hits the end of me. Again and again he bottoms out, tearing me apart in the most exquisite way.

I'm still so swollen and sensitive from my first orgasm that it doesn't take much for him to wind me up again.

"Fucking love this pussy. Want to stay buried deep inside of you for the rest of my life. You want that too, Josephine?"

"Yes, yes… Reed!" The coil snaps and I feel my pussy convulse around his cock again and again. Reed reaches down and rubs my clit, causing me to jerk and spasm beneath him, one orgasm rolling into another.

"So beautiful, sweetheart. Love watching you come. You're gorgeous."

I feel our juices leaking out of me, trickling down my ass and soaking the sheets. Reed pulls out of me and slips two fingers deep inside my cunt, scooping out my honey before rubbing it in between my breasts.

"Push your tits together, Josephine. Make them nice and tight for me."

I do as he says, hot liquid pooling in my belly again at his words. God, I can't imagine coming again, but I'm impossibly turned on right now. He straddles me and strokes his cock once, twice, and then shoves his length in between my breasts.

I open my mouth and suck the head of his cock each time he thrusts forward.

"Shit, Josephine, you like that? Like when I fuck your big tits?"

"Ahhh, yes," I manage to moan.

"Me too, baby. I'm so close already. Squeeze your tits, Josephine. Pinch your nipples. Do it now, love."

I do as he says, playing with my breasts as he glides in and out of me. My thighs start trembling and I don't understand how I can be on the edge of an orgasm after coming so many times already. And yet...

"Oh! Oh God, Reed...ohmygod..."

I squeeze my thighs together again and again, clenching my pussy to try and find some relief. When I pinch my nipples, an unexpected orgasm rolls through my body, causing me to arch my back and dig my fingers into my tits.

"Jesus, Josephine, are you coming right now?"

I cry out, unable to answer him in words.

He grunts and pulls out, still straddling me, and strokes his cock twice before shooting hot cum all over my chest. He's marked me. It's dirty and primal and the hottest thing I've ever experienced.

Every cell in my body throbs as I continue to shake from my powerful orgasm. Reed flops down on the bed next to me with his eyes closed, panting and sweating. We lay next to each other on our backs, both coming down from the intense high we just experienced.

Finally, Reed breaks the silence.

"That was incredible. So fucking hot. Jesus." He turns his head to look at me. Reaching out, he traces along my jaw, down my neck, and over my shoulder. "So beautiful," he murmurs more to himself than to me.

Reed pulls me into his side and arranges us so my arm is flung over his chest and my head is resting on his muscled arm beneath me.

"I'm going to get you all messy," I say, referring to the cum he sprayed all over me.

"Don't care. Need to hold you, sweetness." He leans over and kisses my forehead. "Besides, that just means we need to shower, right?" I feel his smile against my skin.

"Mmhm. That sounds lovely. But I need to recover first. I don't think I can stand."

He chuckles and pulls me in closer, wrapping his arms around me and hugging me to his chest.

Long moments pass by, but we don't move an inch. Finally, Reed's cell phone beeps. He groans, his scratchy voice letting me know he was half asleep. I love that we wore each other out so much.

"That's my alarm," he mutters. "I should get up and wash up before picking up Kayla." Reed doesn't budge, despite his claim.

I poke him in the side, giggling when he twitches. "I'll make you a deal. You hop in the shower first, then go get Kayla. I'll warm up the Italian we never got around to eating last night. We can have leftovers for breakfast?"

"Pasta before nine in the morning?" Reed asks with a grin.

"Um, yeah! I personally think it's better in the morning than in the evening."

Reed laughs, brushing a kiss to my forehead. "Then clearly, I've been missing out."

He gives me one more kiss then gets out of bed. Moments later, I hear the water running.

Reed is out the door in under fifteen minutes. Ugh. Men. It must be nice to rinse off, comb your fingers through your hair, throw on some clothes, and be good to go for the day. I will require a bit more to get me up and at 'em this morning.

Thirty minutes later, I'm dressed in my favorite leggings and sweatshirt, humming to myself as I take out the chicken alfredo and lasagna from the fridge. The phone rings, startling me like it does every dang time. Who still has a landline these days?

I reach for it, then pull my hand back. Whoever it is, isn't calling for me. I could take a message, but it feels like I'm overstepping somehow. I don't know. I just don't want to screw things up.

I let the phone ring, focusing my attention back on the food. Reed's answering machine plays the automated message, saying no one is home. I try to ignore it. It's not my place to be listening in on voice mails.

But then I hear a woman's voice.

"Reed! First of all, why is this landline still connected? I couldn't reach you on your cell, so I thought I'd try this number just for fun." The woman sighs, but I can sense the fondness in her tone. "Secondly, I wanted to check in about the nanny. Is she still a terror?"

Ouch. That stings.

"I know I said to give her some time, but if you're still stressed, I can come back home and help out. I miss you."

She misses him? Who is this woman?

"Anyway, you're probably working. Just wanted to call and say I love you and I worry about you. Call me back!"

The message ends with a beep.

I stand in the kitchen, trembling from head to toe. Reed was talking about me behind my back? He told some woman I was being a terror?

No, not *some* woman. Whoever she is, she's clearly important to Reed. She misses him and she loves him. She offered to move in and help.

Reality slaps me in the face, sending me reeling back until I bump up against the counter.

He's seeing someone else.

No. That's not... no.

But then who is she?

Tears blur my vision, and I can't seem to take a full breath. This doesn't make sense. None of it does.

What did I get myself into?

My thoughts are racing just as fast as my heart, and suddenly, I think I might be sick.

I run upstairs to my room, shutting the door. My bed is still made, a poignant reminder of where I slept last night.

My head is spinning, my lungs are on fire from trying to take deep breaths, and my stomach twists violently, making me double over. I stumble to the bed, curling up in a ball. What the hell am I going to do?

I can't leave Kayla. I won't. But Reed... Can I really stay here, under the same roof, knowing I'm just some girl on the side?

A wretched sob shakes my body. This can't be happening.

I hear a car door shut, then footsteps trail up the driveway. The back door opens a few moments later, and I curl further into myself, not wanting to face Reed.

"Josephine?" Reed calls out.

My heart lurches in my chest, more tears wrung from the depths of my sorrow. What am I going to say to him?

"Kayla wanted to stay longer, so we have the morning to ourselves."

I choke out another sob, wishing so damn bad I could go back in time and unhear that message. But, no, I don't want that either. I don't want to be with a cheater or a liar. I just want Reed. I want him to be mine and only mine.

"Jo? Where are you?"

Reed climbs up the stairs, and I hear his footsteps drawing closer, closer, closer until they block the light from underneath my door.

"Are you in here?" Reed knocks on the door softly. A sniffle escapes, but I bury my face in my pillow to try and muffle it. "Josephine?" He sounds alarmed. "Baby, what's wrong? Are you crying?"

The knob turns, and I slam my eyes shut, not wanting to deal with any of this right now.

Chapter 10

Reed

I open the door to Josephine's room, the sound of her tears propelling me forward. She's curled up in the center of the bed, her arms wrapped around her body in a protective hold while she buries her face into her pillow.

"Josephine," I choke out, kneeling on the bed. I reach for her, but she shuffles away from me. *Fuck, that hurts.*

"I know, okay?" she says in a broken voice.

"You know... what? Talk to me, baby. What's wrong?"

I ball my fists up instead of reaching out for her again. I want to pull her into my arms and tip her chin up so she has to look at me. I want her blue eyes on mine when she tells what made her so upset. I can't stand being this far away from her, but I don't want to upset her further.

Josephine is still and quiet, only a few sniffles here and there punctuating the silence. Each one tears at my heart, not knowing what happened. I left her this morning with a smile on her face and came home to a broken, red-headed angel in tears. What the hell happened in such a short amount of time?

"Voicemail," she finally whispers.

"Voicemail..." I repeat. "You left me a voicemail?" I dig around in my pants pocket for my phone but can't find it. I check my jacket, but it's not there either. "Shit, I don't think I even brought my phone with me to get Kayla, so I missed your message. Can you tell me what it said?"

A few more sniffles, and then Josephine takes a shuddering breath. She still has her back facing me, but at least the tears have slowed down.

"Go check your answering machine," she says softly.

My brow furrows and I grit my teeth. Why is she being so cryptic? Is whatever voicemail all that bad? I can't even remember the last person who used it other than a random solicitor. I have to have a registered home number for the university, but no one typically calls me.

"Okay," I finally answer. I would rather have Josephine tell me what's so upsetting, but if listening to a damn voicemail is going to clear things up, I can at least do that much.

Getting off the bed, I run a hand through my hair, then look over my shoulder at Josephine. She's on her side, facing away from me, her curvy little body shaking as she gets her tears under control. Jesus, my chest, my heart, my entire being *aches* knowing she's in pain and won't let me help.

Walking out to the kitchen, I see the two takeout containers from last night sitting on the counter, along with plates and silverware. So she was getting breakfast ready when someone called. But who?

I glare at the answering machine, annoyed that it exists. The red message light flashes, mocking me, and I hit it rather forcefully with my thumb. I just want to clear this shit up so Josephine and I can pick up where we left off this morning.

"Reed! First of all, why is this landline still connected? I couldn't reach you on your cell, so I thought I'd try this number just for fun. Secondly, I wanted to check in about the nanny. Is she still a terror? I know I said to give her some time, but if you're still stressed, I can come back home and help out. I miss you. Anyway, you're probably working. Just wanted to call and say I love you and I worry about you. Call me back!"

"Emmaline," I mutter, rubbing my eyes so hard I see spots.

"Is that her name?"

I snap my head up, looking at Josephine. She's in leggings that hug her curves and that adorable cat sweatshirt she loves so much. I want to pull her down onto the couch and snuggle, and also rip her clothes off so I can have another taste.

Before any of that, however, we need to have a chat.

"Yes," I answer. Josephine's shoulders drop, her blue eyes filling with tears as she folds in on herself. "Emmaline is my sister."

Josephine rolls her eyes and snorts out a humorless laugh. "Right. Is that what you told her about me, too? That I'm not your side chick, I'm just your sister?"

I rear my head back, shocked by the bitterness in her tone. My Josephine isn't like that. She's sweet, sunshiney, and pure.

"No, I–"

"Oh, so you just didn't tell her anything then? Were you planning to get rid of me before she moved back in?"

"Josephine, if you let me explain, I–"

"I'm not stupid!" she yells, crossing her arms over her chest. "Just because I gave you my virginity doesn't mean I'm some naive, love-struck fool who will just believe anything you say. Sorry to be such a *terror.*"

She heaves out a breath, then winds up for another lashing. I've had enough of this, however.

I grab the phone from its cradle then stomp toward Josephine. Wrapping an arm around her waist, I pick up my woman, kicking and screaming, and haul her into the living room. I set Josephine down on her feet, then crowd her against the wall, not letting her escape.

She glares at me, her blue eyes sharp as icicles and just as cold. Her little fist pounds on my chest a few times, but she doesn't try to break free. My sweetness wants me to fight for her, and that's exactly what I plan to do.

"Let me explain," I murmur to Josephine, my voice low and commanding.

Her jaw tightens and her nostrils flare, but she doesn't say anything.

I cup the side of her neck with one hand, my thumb stroking along her jaw, wanting to ease her tension. Despite her anger and hurt, Josephine leans into my touch. I keep her pinned against the wall with my body, holding her steady and forcing her to look up at me.

I have the phone in my other hand, and I dial my sister's number before putting the call on speaker. Josephine's eyes narrow, then widen when Emmaline answers.

"Did you lose your cell phone or something?" Emmaline asks, getting straight to the point. Too bad I have a different point I'm looking to make.

"I have someone I'd like you to meet."

Josephine's breath catches in her throat, and she rolls her lips in a nervous gesture.

"Uh... okay...?" Emmaline sounds as confused as Josephine looks.

"Kayla's new nanny, and my future wife, Josephine, seems to think my heart belongs to someone else."

Both women gasp at my words.

"Ohmygod, ohmygod, REED!" Emmaline exclaims, recovering faster than Josephine. "I'm so happy for you! Wait, she doesn't know you love her? What is your problem? Why haven't you locked that down yet? She's been living with you guys for weeks now. *Weeks*!"

My eyes never leave Josephine's. Her lower lip trembles and she blinks away more tears. I lean down, brushing my lips across her forehead.

"I never said I was a smart man," I tell Josephine and Em.

Emmaline snorts, making Josephine's lip twitch up in a smile. "Um, yeah, you pretty much exude big brain energy. You're a freaking dean of a freaking college."

I grunt and roll my eyes, but inside I'm thrilled that Josephine seems amused by my sister. "Well, when it comes to relationships, I'll be the first to admit I'm completely lost. I could use your help to clarify one thing, though."

"Only if you name your firstborn after me," Em deadpans.

Josephine coughs out a surprised laugh, and I grin down at her, nuzzling into the side of her neck.

"Is she listening in? Reed, is she right there with you?! Why didn't you tell me? She must think I'm so rude. God, you're the worst sometimes."

Josephine laughs more heartily this time, and I close my eyes, loving the sound.

"Please excuse my brother. I'm Emmaline, the much younger sister to this big lug."

I growl, but it's all in jest. I don't care what Emmaline calls me as long as Josephine keeps looking at me like she is now. Like she trusts me again and wants to build a future with me.

"I'm Josephine," she replies, darting her eyes up to meet mine.

"Josephine. I love that name! Oh, my god, I think I know what happened." Emmaline is often up in the clouds, making connections and having conversations in her head. Sometimes she blurts things out that seem random but are actually very insightful. "My voicemail must have sounded bad, huh?"

"You could say that again," I mutter.

"Oh, hush. I'm not apologizing to you. But Josephine, I'm so sorry if I made you doubt my brother or made things messy. I'm so happy he's found someone to tolerate him."

I grunt again, making Jo laugh.

"For real, though," Em continues. "He's one of the good ones. I can't wait to meet you on my next visit, Josephine! Give Kayla a hug and kiss from me."

"Thanks, Em," I say. "I'm going to hang up now and show my woman exactly how much she means to me."

"Ew! I don't want to know!"

Josephine laughs, and I hang up the phone, tossing it somewhere over my shoulder before claiming her lips.

I kiss her softly at first, with all the tenderness I should have shown her from the beginning. Josephine rolls her body against mine, her hands sliding up, up, up my chest before diving into my hair, pulling me closer.

I open up for my sweet, sexy Josephine, letting her taste and explore what belongs to her. My hips jerk when she nips my tongue, and she moans before doing it again. I trace her curves with my large hands, squeezing her hips, cupping her breasts, and pinching her rock-hard nipples. The answering cry of pleasure makes my cock throb.

Reluctantly, I lean back, collecting the last threads of my sanity. Josephine is panting, her eyes glazed over with lust.

"Do you believe me now, baby? You're it for me. Told you last night. Told you this morning. And I'll tell you again every damn day of our lives. You're the only one, Josephine. I love you."

Her eyes water, but she nods her head, giving me a shy smile. "I'm sorry I freaked out. I thought it was too good to be true, you know? It doesn't make any sense for you to want me."

Her words pain me. I tuck a few strands of her bright red hair behind her ears, then press a kiss to her temple, breathing in her sweet strawberry scent. "I want every goddamn thing with you," I vow. She has no idea I've had a ring burning a hole in my pocket for the last five days. "I want your body beneath mine every night. I want your laughter filling this house. I want your smiles, your burdens, your fears, your history... all of you. God, Josephine, I don't know how I managed to breathe before you came into my life. I can't do it without you now. I need you, sweetness."

"Reed..." Her endless blue eyes hold such hope and awe. I want her to always look at me like that.

"Let me show you," I whisper against the corner of her lips before pressing a kiss there. "Let me remind you how good we are together. How perfect." I kiss the other corner of her mouth then trail my lips down her neck. "Let me take care of you, baby. That's all I want to do for the rest of my life."

Josephine nods her head, winding her arms around my neck. "I love you, Reed Landis," she murmurs seconds before her lips meet mine.

"Thank fuck," I growl.

Josephine laughs at my outburst, then squeals as I lift her up and toss her over my shoulder. Time to make my woman so delirious with pleasure she never thinks about doubting me again.

Chapter 11

Josephine

His sister.

God, I'm such a spaz.

I don't have time to think about what a fool I made of myself when Reed is carrying me through the house over his shoulder like a caveman. I love it.

I think he's going to stop in his bedroom, but he keeps going straight through into the attached bathroom. Reed sets me down in front of the shower, his lips finding mine as his hands tear at my clothes.

We already took showers not long ago, but this is a different kind of cleansing. We're washing away confusion, doubt, mistakes, and misunderstandings until there's nothing left but the two of us.

Reed rips his clothes off in record time and is naked before me. He's stunning. I love his broad shoulders and defined pecs, the corded muscles in his arms, all of his strength that he uses to protect and comfort me. And then there's his cock. Without even thinking, I lick my lips.

"See something you like?"

I look up, and Reed is grinning at me.

"Yeah," I say before pulling him down for a kiss.

It's just as explosive as always, our tongues warring for control as his hands stroke my body up and down. He cups my ass and lifts me, walking us towards the shower, never breaking the kiss.

Only when he sets me down do we both come up for air.

"Fuck, baby. I missed you. Missed these lips." He kisses me again, short and sweet. "Missed your skin." He kisses across my jaw, down my neck, over my collar bone. "Missed these perfect breasts." He sucks one of my breasts in his mouth while flicking the nipple on my other breast with his thumb. Everything he does drives me crazy with want, with need.

"It's only been like an hour since…"

"Don't care," he growls. "Missed you. Fucking *need* you."

"Yes…" I moan, knowing exactly what he means. It's primal, the way I need this man.

Reed kisses lower, kneeling before me. His hands rest on my hips, guiding me backward so I'm leaning against the shower wall.

"Need your taste on my tongue before I fuck you nice and deep," he grunts.

I moan at his words, loving the dirty way he's talking to me. He nips at my hip bone and blazes a trail of kisses to my other hip bone, where he sucks and nips the skin. I feel his hands massaging my ass, then gripping lower on my thighs.

Reed guides one leg over his shoulder, giving him complete access to my soaked pussy. I feel exposed, but not in a bad way. I should be embarrassed, but I'm not. He looks like he's about to go out of his mind with need, and I feel the same.

He turns his head and sinks his teeth into the thigh slung over his shoulder, kissing away the sting.

"Are you wet for me, baby?"

I nod and dig my fingers into his hair, urging him forward. He flattens his tongue and runs it from my entrance to my clit. Again. Again. I buck my hips and moan his name. Reed strokes his tongue deep inside my channel, causing my pussy to pulse around him and release a wave of wetness. Reed growls and the vibrations echo off every nerve in my body.

He pulls his tongue out and thrusts it back in, fucking me with his mouth while rubbing my clit with his thumb. It's almost too much. I'm getting close already. So close…

Reed withdraws his tongue and finger, and I cry out at the loss.

"I've got you, baby. I'll always take care of you."

He licks my tight ball of nerves, drawing figure eights with his tongue, over and over. And then he slams two fingers in my hole and my body jerks, back arching off the wall.

Reed moves his other hand from my hip to my stomach, spreading his fingers out over my tummy, keeping me pinned to the wall while also intensifying the pressure I feel building again in my lower abdomen.

"D-don't stop, please..." He pumps his fingers faster, curling them up and hitting my most sensitive spot. My thighs jerk together and he strokes the spot again.

Reed alternates between fast, slow, hard, and soft licks. Then, he sucks my little nub into his mouth and softly bites down. That's it. My orgasm rips through me.

He replaces his fingers with his tongue, lapping up all of my cum as my pussy convulses around him, squeezing his tongue as he massages my walls. I can feel the stress melt off my bones and pool in my core, dripping out of me as Reed sucks it all in.

The last of my orgasm fades and I slump against Reed. He stands up and kisses me, long and deep, slow and passionate. I taste myself on him and it's so fucking hot. He slides his hands up to my hips and I throw my arms around his neck, forcing the kiss to go deeper.

He finally breaks the kiss and nuzzles my neck, kissing my shoulder. He lifts his head and rests it on my forehead. We're both breathing heavily, sharing the same air, the same intensity.

"Goddamn, baby. Love watching you come apart in my hands, in my mouth. Fucking beautiful."

Before I can respond, he captures my mouth in a frantic kiss, all teeth and tongue and fire while guiding me back against the wall. He breaks the kiss to lift me into his arms. My legs automatically wrap around his hips and I feel his hard cock rub up and down my slit.

"Yes," I moan, grinding against him.

He growls but continues to slide his length through my folds, not entering me. His cock slides across my clit, winding that coil deep within tighter and tighter with each stroke.

I feel his mouth roam over my neck, chest, nipples, and everywhere in between. The heat of his tongue and the sting of his teeth peppering my skin and setting my nerves on fire. My fingers tangle in his hair as I hold on for dear life.

Finally, *finally,* he thrusts his cock deep inside me while biting down on my nipple. The coil snaps and I come instantly, pulsing and shaking in his arms. My scream catches in my throat. I forget to breathe.All I can do is drown in wave after wave of pleasure as it washes over me and leaks out from between my thighs.

"Jesus Christ, Josephine. Love when you come on my dick. So fucking beautiful, baby. You feel so good." Reed licks my neck and nibbles at my pulse point. I feel his lips brushing the shell of my ear. "Breathe, baby girl. Take a breath for me."

I drag air into my lungs, the oxygen pulling pleasure along with it while traveling into my bloodstream and coursing throughout my body. I hear Reed chuckle as he pulls my earlobe through his teeth.

All I can do is moan at this point.

"I have to move, baby."

I nod, and he surges forward, setting a punishing pace. His fingers tighten around my thighs as he holds me in place, pounding into me again and again. It hurts so good, feeling his cock stretch me, his fingers bruise me, his teeth sink into me.

I tilt my head back and he covers my mouth with his, swallowing my cries in an all-consuming kiss. He rests his forehead on mine and grunts with each thrust of his hips. I didn't think I had anything left in me, but the pressure is building again in my core, quickly overwhelming me as my legs start to shake.

Reed pulls his head back enough to look me in the eyes. His gaze is so intense, but I can't look away. "Come for me, Josephine. One more time, baby girl." I close my eyes as I reach the point of no return. "Eyes on me, Josephine. I want to watch you come."

I snap my eyes open right as pleasure overtakes my body. Reed's cock swells inside of me and explodes as another wave of pleasure vibrates through me, through him, through us, breathing, pulsing together as one.

"*Fuck*, Josephine, Josephine..." he chants my name over and over as the last of our orgasm slips away, dripping down between us.

The moment lasts forever. We never break eye contact, and I can see every emotion Reed is feeling, just like I know he can see all of me at this moment, so raw and unfiltered.

Reed sets me down, keeping one hand around my waist while his other hand goes behind me, bracing himself on the wall. We're both still shaking, and Reed is as unsteady as I am on my feet right now.

He tucks me into his chest, resting his forehead on the wall, covering me with his entire body, like he's shielding me from everything outside of this moment. I place a gentle kiss on his chest before burying my head there and wrapping my arms around his waist.

"I've got you, my sweet Josephine. I'm right here," he murmurs over and over.

Reed holds me together while I find all the pieces of his heart, keeping them as my own. I feel complete in every way, fully seen, fully understood, and fully loved.

My knees wobble, and Reed tightens his hold on me, then shuts off the water. He helps me out of the shower and dries me off, then scoops me up and carries me to bed.

"I love you so much," Reed whispers, kissing the tip of my nose.

I smile, so happy my heart might just burst. His green eyes twinkle with a joy I've never seen before. It makes everything about him look more vibrant, more alive. Like he can breathe easier, just like he told me.

"I love you more, Serious Mr. McEducator Man."

Reed grins at me, his playful look sending shockwaves throughout my body. "We might need to come up with a different nickname if you're going to keep making me smile."

"Hmm," I muse, tapping my chin. "How about–"

"Uncle Reed! Jo Jo! Where are you guys?"

"Shit, I forgot Mrs. Brady said she would drop Kayla off at noon."

My stomach drops, and I scramble out of bed. Reed pulls me back, giving me a quick kiss before hopping out of bed and throwing on some clothes.

"Don't panic, baby," he says with a smile. "Kayla and I talked this morning about everything. I don't ever want to hide our relationship."

"Are you sure? This is such a big step, and I haven't been here very long in the grand scheme of things, and–"

Reed plants one knee on the bed, leaning over me and caging me in with his arms. "I've never been more sure of anything in my life, sweetness. You're mine. You belong in this family. You belong right here with Kayla and me." He kisses me then stands up again. "Grab a shirt of mine and meet us downstairs. I promise everything will be okay."

I crawl out of bed, putting on a pair of Reed's sweatpants and an oversized t-shirt. He opens the door just in time for Kayla to come crashing through. She blows past Reed and hops on the bed, beaming her brilliant smile at me as she jumps up and down.

I look over at Reed, who has a grin plastered on his face, then back at Kayla, who has a matching grin.

"Finally!" Kayla says, flopping down on the bed. "I thought I'd have to spend the night again at Megan's for you guys to figure your stuff out."

My eyes are bugging out of my head as I stare at the clever six-year-old. I'm sure she doesn't know what we were up to while she was at her slumber party, but she's smart enough to sense that the dynamic between Reed and me has changed.

"Are you... okay with your uncle and I dating?"

"Dating?" Kayla scrunches up her nose then throws a disapproving glare at Reed. "I thought you said you wanted to marry her."

I choke out a cough, then smile when Kayla giggles. "Yes, Reed, you seem to be telling a lot of people about me being your wife, but I don't see a ring," I say with a wink.

My tummy fills with drunken bats once again, not sure if I should joke about getting engaged. It's a huge step. One that I want more than anything, but I would never pressure these two into something like that so soon.

"Dammit, haven't I proposed yet?"

I shake my head no, not sure how to take his response. Green eyes sparkle at me, then focus on Kayla.

Reed helps Kayla off the bed and whispers something to her. She claps her hands and nods enthusiastically before skipping out of the room.

"What was that about?" I ask, walking into Reed's outstretched arms. He wraps himself around me and rocks us back and forth, pressing a kiss to my forehead.

"It's all part of my big romantic gesture," he whispers.

I snort a laugh. "I don't think it counts if you have to tell me it's a romantic gesture."

Reed frowns, and he's so adorable, I have to bite his bottom lip. He grunts, then cups the back of my head, angling me so he can slide his tongue deep inside my mouth.

"You guys!" Kayla's impatient little voice breaks the moment, and she clears her throat rather unsubtly.

I blush and bury my face in Reed's chest. He chuckles then nudges my head up. Reed takes a step back, getting down on one knee.

My hands cover my mouth as I stare at him, not believing what I'm seeing. He motions for Kayla to come stand next to him, and she practically floats over to his side. Her glittering eyes meet mine, and my heart melts all over again for this little girl. So strong and brave and incredibly kind.

"Jo Jo," she addresses me in all seriousness. "Uncle Reed and I decided we want to keep you. Forever."

The first tears fall, but I'm quick to wipe them away. I don't want to miss a single second of this.

"Forever is a long time," I say. "Are you sure you're up for that?"

"Yes," they both answer immediately.

"Josephine, my sweet girl," Reed says, looping his fingers around my left wrist and pulling it down toward him. Kayla produces a little black velvet box from behind her back, opening it up and handing Reed the gorgeous diamond ring inside. Reed places it on my ring finger, kissing the diamond. "Will you complete this little family?"

I sniffle, looking down at the ring and then up at Reed and Kayla, matching green eyes pleading with me to agree. Gah, these two. They're my whole heart.

"I can't cook," I tell them.

"Me either," Kayla says, making Reed laugh.

"And I'm not a very good maid," I add.

"Uncle Reed can hire more maids."

"Besides," Reed interrupts. "I don't want a chef or a housekeeper. I want *you*, Josephine. Just as you are. So what do you say? Will you be our family?"

"Come on, Jo Jo! Say yes!"

I have to swallow the lump in my throat to get any sound out. "Yes," I squeak. The word hardly passes my lips before I'm being tackled onto the bed, both Reed and Kayla piling on top of me. I tickle Kayla, who giggles and pinches Reed's side. He growls playfully, rolling over and tickling Kayla with me.

After a few blissful moments, Kayla settles on one side of me, resting her head on my stomach. Reed flops down on my other side, tugging both Kayla and me closer. The three of us stay cocooned in warmth and happiness until Kayla dozes off, her soft snores making me smile.

"God, I love you so much," Reed whispers. He lifts my left hand, inspecting my ring. "I can't wait for you to be my wife."

I smile up at him. "I love you, Reed. Thank you for giving me a place to call home. Right here." I rest my hand over his heart, loving how my ring catches the light.

"Thank you for putting up with me until I figured my shit out."

I laugh, then sigh contentedly when Reed tucks me back into his side. Kayla is passed out next to me, her hand tangled in my hair from where she was playing with it. I love these two with everything in me. I didn't think it was possible to get everything I've ever desired, but now I know happily ever afters are real. So very real.

Epilogue

Reed

"Happy birthday, dear Maya, happy birthday to you!"

Our five-year-old looks around the backyard at the friends and family gathered for her birthday, her red hair shining in the sunlight. She gives me a big grin, showcasing her two front teeth, or lack thereof. Maya lost both of them yesterday, and the tooth fairy was very generous this time around.

"Isn't her smile the cutest?" Josephine whispers right next to me.

"It is," I agree, kissing her temple. "But I think the tooth fairy should keep it to spare change instead of cash. Maya is going to be pulling all of her teeth to get more money," I tease.

Josephine smacks me playfully, and I grab her wrist, lifting it and turning so I can brush my lips against her pulse point.

Maya blows out her candles, and everyone cheers. Kayla hugs her little sister, then swipes her finger through the frosting of Maya's piece of cake. I laugh, and Josephine sighs, though the smile never drops from her face.

Our girls are best friends, but Kayla loves to rile Maya up. Good thing Maya is as bubbly and forgiving as her mother.

Josephine and I got married a few months after Kayla and I proposed. We legally adopted Kayla as our daughter and had Maya shortly after. She has Josephine's fiery red hair and bright smile. I love my family to pieces, each of my girls filling up my heart with more love and joy than I knew possible.

My wife snuggles up against me, and I wrap an arm around her, tucking her further into my side. She rests her head on my shoulder while I look across our backyard at the happy couples and kids running around.

Dylan and Sarah are over on the swings with their kids, Evan and Eleanor. Sarah just found out she's pregnant with her third, and the two could not be more thrilled. I never thought the cocky professor, who also happens to be one of my best friends, would settle down. Then again, I never thought my life would turn out the way it did either.

Sarah's best friend, Faye, has become part of the family over the years. Her husband, Jasper, absolutely adores her and their two children. I search for them, smiling when I see Faye whispering something in her daughter Kate's ear. Faye hands her a cupcake and puts her finger over her lips, indicating Kate should be quiet.

Josephine is watching now, too. Faye taps Jasper's left shoulder, then ducks right as he turns, giving Kate the perfect shot. The little girl lobs the cupcake at her dad, who looks shocked for half a second, then bursts out laughing. Jasper catches the cupcake and starts chasing after his wife and daughter, with Gray, their son, close behind.

I laugh along with Josephine, then spin her around in my arms, dipping her low and hovering my mouth above hers.

"Love you, my sweet girl," I whisper.

"Love you more, my charming husband," she murmurs.

I taste the words on her lips, drinking down her love and devotion, and giving her all of mine in return. I didn't think I could love Josephine any more than I already do, but I know I will tomorrow. And the next day. And the day after that. All the way into eternity.

THE END

Connect with me!

Check out my website, cameronhart.net[1], for sneak previews on my latest projects.

Follow me on social media:

Facebook Page - facebook.com/cameronhartauthor
Instagram - instagram.com/cameron.hart.author
TikTok - tiktok.com/@author.cameron.hart
Goodreads - goodreads.com/16081533.Cameron_Hart
Bookbub - bookbub.com/authors/cameron-hart

---

1. https://cameronhart.net/

www.ingramcontent.com/pod-product-compliance
Lightning Source LLC
Chambersburg PA
CBHW021957170726
47994CB00021B/854